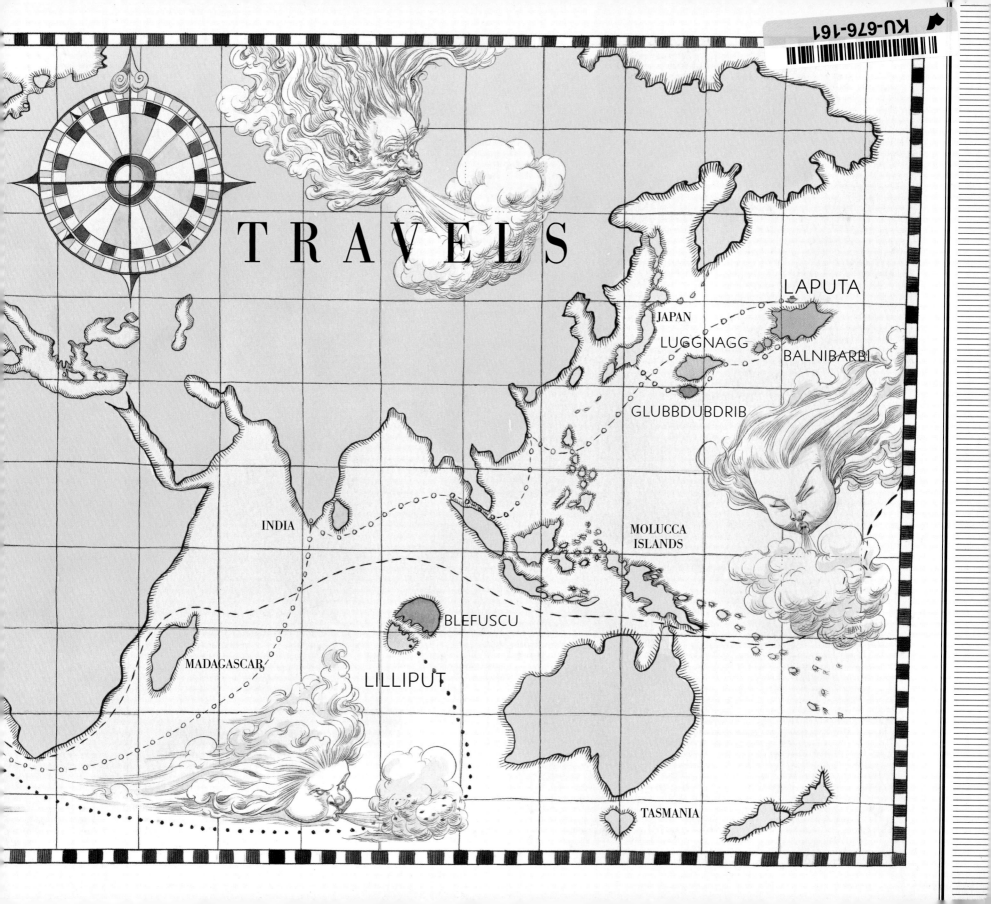

TRAVELS

LAPUTA

JAPAN

LUGGNAGG

BALNIBARBI

GLUBBDUBDRIB

INDIA

MOLUCCA
ISLANDS

BLEFUSCU

MADAGASCAR

LILLIPUT

TASMANIA

My name is Gulliver. Lemuel Gulliver. I live quietly here at Redriff, in south London. Today has been a very important day for me. I came back from the stable, where I had been having my usual daily conversation with my horses, and decided that for the first time in five years I would allow my wife to sit down to dinner with me. Of course, she had to stay at the furthest end of the table, and I kept a nosegay of scented herbs with me the whole time, to ward off any smells. But I did actually let her speak a few words to me. I now think I might even be able to bear a visit from one of our neighbours soon, but I am not yet sure.

I have also decided that it is time I told my own story, before anyone else presumes to tell it for me – I have heard rumours that this may be the case. Fortunately I have an excellent memory – and a reputation for complete honesty – so you may trust every detail of what you are about to read.

# GULLIVER

ILLUSTRATED BY

# CHRIS RIDDELL

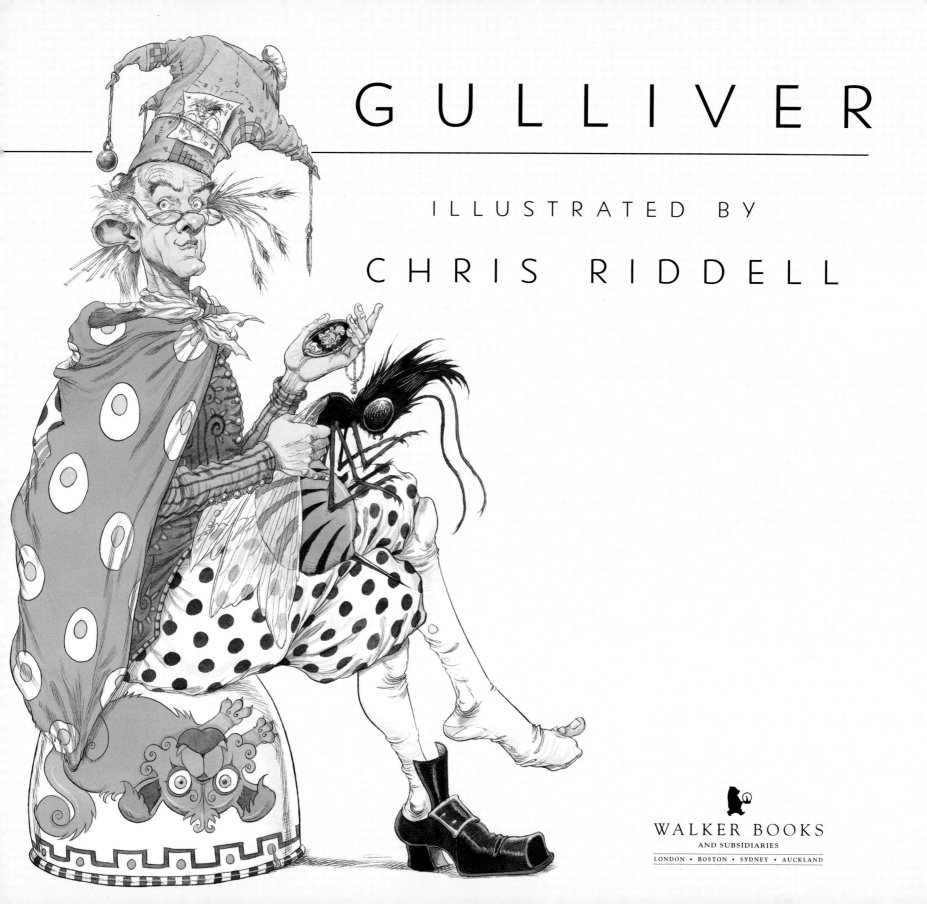

WALKER BOOKS
AND SUBSIDIARIES
LONDON · BOSTON · SYDNEY · AUCKLAND

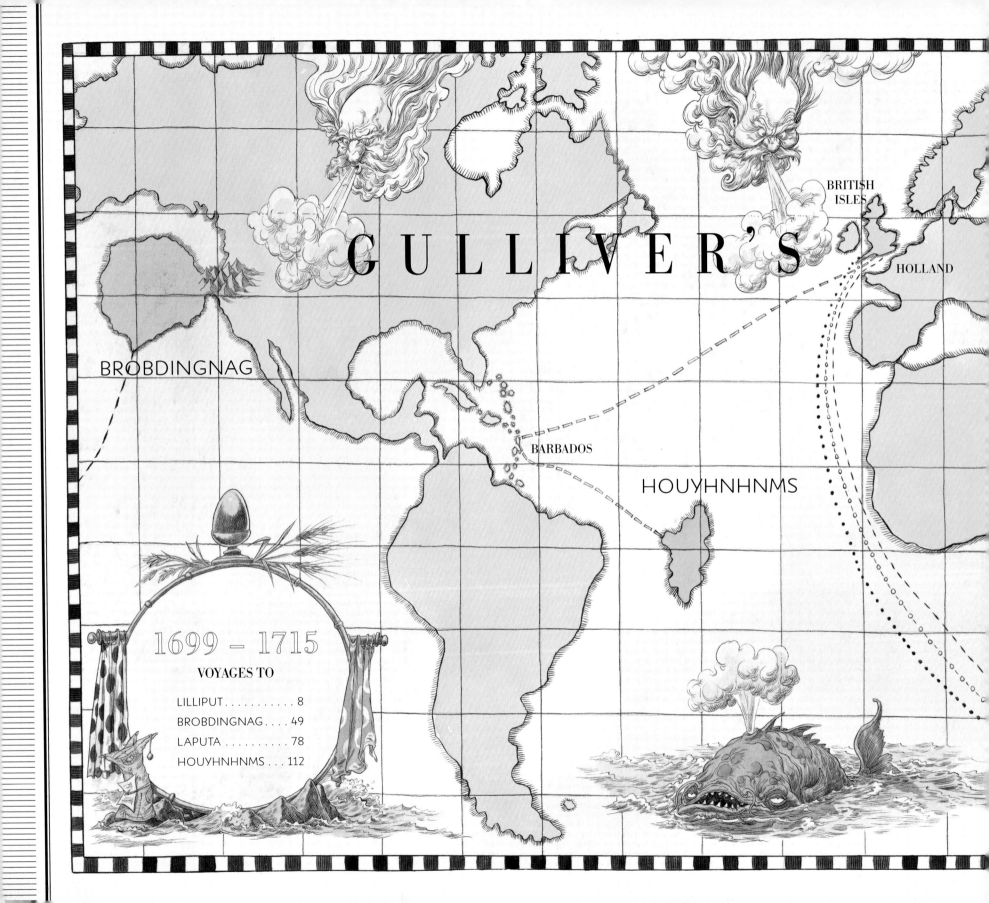

# GULLIVER'S

BRITISH
ISLES

HOLLAND

BROBDINGNAG

BARBADOS

HOUYHNHNMS

## 1699 – 1715

### VOYAGES TO

# A VOYAGE TO LILLIPUT

I was born in Nottinghamshire and was sent to Cambridge University when I was fourteen years old. Three years later I began training as a surgeon, first in London and afterwards in Leyden in the Netherlands. I made several voyages as a ship's surgeon, but grew tired of the sea and decided to set up as a doctor in Wapping, where I moved with my wife and children. However, business did not go well and I again took a post as a ship's surgeon.

The ship I was employed on, the *Antelope*, sailed from Bristol on 4 May 1699, bound for the South Seas. In early November a violent storm blew the ship off course, and we ended up somewhere to the north-west of Tasmania. On 5 November the ship was driven onto a rock and wrecked. Six of us managed to escape in the lifeboat, but shortly afterwards it was overturned in a sudden gale. I swam as best I could and eventually found myself in shallow water within sight of land. I staggered ashore and, completely exhausted, fell asleep immediately.

When I awoke, it was just daylight. I was lying on my back and tried to sit up, only to find that I was stuck fast. I could not even move my head. It seemed that I was tied to the ground by hundreds of pieces of string.

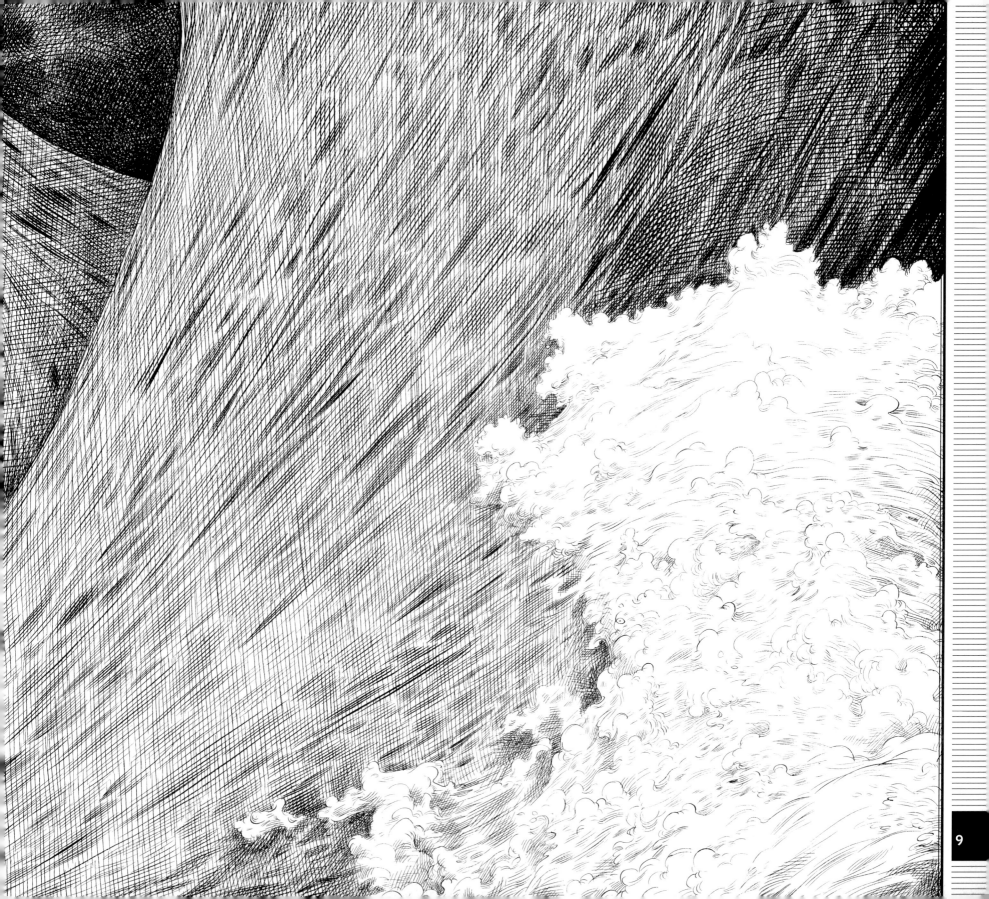

9

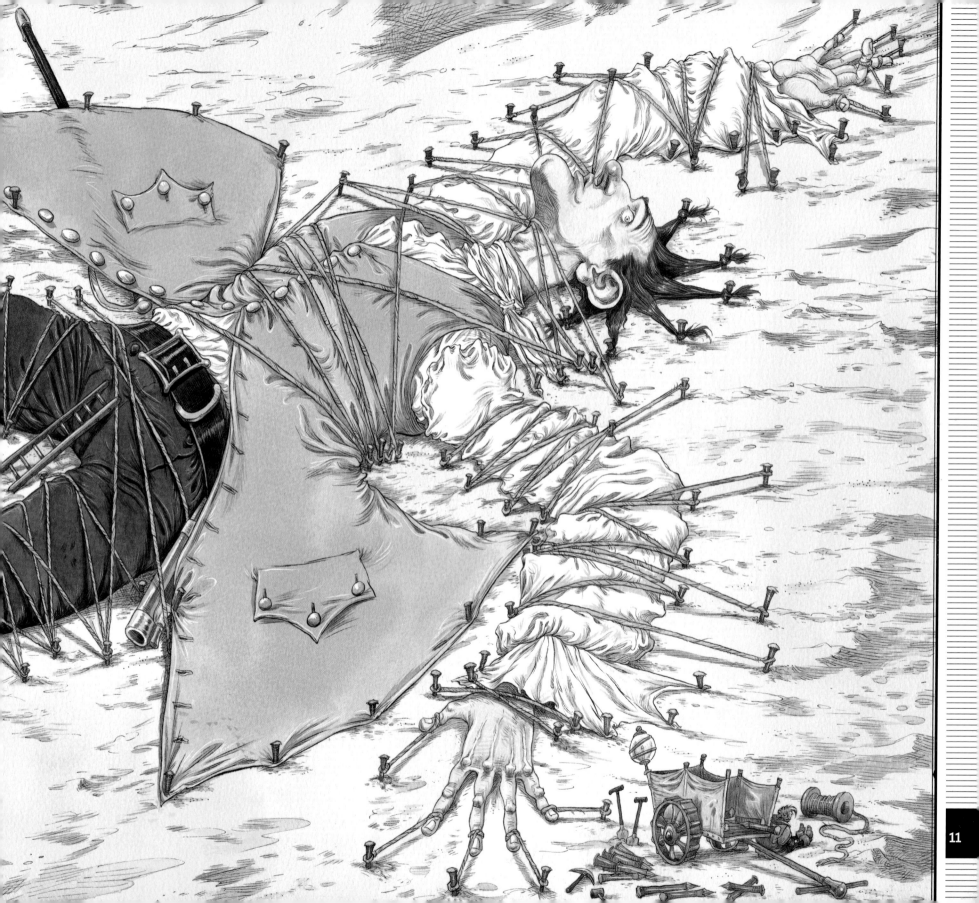

Eventually, as the sun was becoming uncomfortably bright and hot, I felt a living thing move up my left leg and onto my body, closely followed by about forty more. The first creature, whatever it was, came to a halt just under my chin, and by peering downwards I found I could just make it out. To my astonishment, what did I see but a miniature human no bigger than my hand, equipped with bow and arrow! In my amazement I let out a loud roar, and all the creatures turned and fled back down my body, some of them falling off in their hurry to get away. They were soon back, however.

Struggling to get loose, I finally managed to free my left arm, and, by pulling violently, loosened the threads tying my hair down, so that I could turn my head a little. I tried to grab a handful of the tiny men but they scurried off again, all yelling at once. Then one of them cried, "Tolgo phonac" and I was instantly bombarded with hundreds of minute arrows, which pricked me like so many needles and hurt terribly. I quickly decided that it might be wise to lie still and try to free myself under cover of night, when I would be able to sneak away. Soon I heard a lot of clattering and banging to my right, and saw that a tall platform was being built. Four of the little creatures climbed up to it and the tallest of them, who seemed to be rather important, made a great long speech directed at me, of which I didn't understand a single word.

12

13

As you might imagine, I was absolutely starving by now and, although it was rather rude of me, I indicated this by pointing vigorously to my mouth. The important person understood immediately, and ordered food to be brought. It was all tiny – I ate three loaves of bread in one mouthful – but delicious. They then brought me wine to drink in what must have been their largest barrels, and some ointment to soothe the pain caused by the arrow wounds. They smeared my wounds with ointment and then loosed the ties on my left side – and not a moment too soon, for all the drink they had given me had filled my bladder to bursting. The creatures on my right side quickly realized what was going to happen and ran clear, turning to gasp in amazement at the gushing torrent I produced. I then gestured as best I could that I would like to be let free, trying to indicate that I would do them no harm, but they refused.

I soon fell deeply asleep (I later discovered that they had put a sleeping potion in the wine) and woke up to find something tickling my nostril, making me sneeze terribly. I found I was being carried on a sort of platform on wheels, drawn by no fewer than fifteen hundred horses.

We stopped near a large city, and my left ankle was bound with chains to the front wall of a building that looked like some sort of temple. At least a hundred thousand people, including someone who was evidently the emperor himself, came out of the city to see me. Thousands of the sightseers clambered up ladders to swarm over my body, causing me considerable irritation, until the emperor forbade it.

When they were sure I was securely chained, my ropes were cut and I was at last able to stand up. You can imagine the commotion that caused. Feeling very down at heart, I turned round and crawled into the temple, where I found I could lie down at full stretch.

When I finally came out again, I found the emperor coming towards me on one of the miniature horses. He ordered me to be given food and drink, and began to speak to me. To see and hear him better, I lay down on my side. He was very smartly dressed and much taller than the people around him, who included ladies in sumptuous dresses, and what appeared to be a number of priests and lawyers. The emperor, priests and lawyers spoke to me for over two hours and I replied in all the languages I could – I am very good at languages and know several – but they couldn't understand me and nor, for that matter, could I understand them.

The court then went off, leaving a large number of guards to keep the crowds away. Some ruffians were impertinent enough to shoot arrows at me as I sat on the ground outside my home. One of the arrows only narrowly missed my left eye. The man in charge of the guards seized six of the ringleaders and decided that the best way to punish them was to hand them over to me. I picked them up, put five of them in my coat pocket and then pretended to be about to eat the sixth. He was terrified, and let out an awful yell. I took out my pocket knife, which frightened them all even more, but then used it to cut the ropes binding the man and put him gently on the ground. I then freed the other five in the same way. The soldiers and the crowd were very impressed by how merciful I had been.

As news of my arrival spread, huge numbers of people came to look at me. They all stopped work and the whole country threatened to grind to a halt. The emperor ordered everyone who had already seen me to go home, saying they could only come near me again if they paid a licence fee. The treasury made a lot of money collecting these fees.

In the meantime, I later learnt, the royal court were discussing what to do with me. They were afraid that I might break free, or eat all the country's food. They thought of starving me to death or poisoning me with their arrows, but then decided that my corpse would be too difficult to get rid of, and would soon start to rot and smell horrible, perhaps even causing a plague.

While the court were arguing, some soldiers came in and told them how kindly I had treated the criminals

who had attacked me. The court were so impressed that they abandoned their plans to get rid of me, and instead decided I should be properly looked after. Each day I was to be fed six cows, forty sheep and lots of bread and wine, paid for by the treasury. Six hundred people were appointed to look after me; three hundred tailors were ordered to make me a suit; and six of the best teachers were to teach me the language.

I soon started my lessons. The emperor himself often came to help. Each time, I begged him for my freedom, but he replied that I must be patient. In any case I would first have to swear an oath of peace and agree to be searched for any weapons.

With my consent, two of the emperor's agents searched me. Here is my translation of their report:

❏ **Item:** Right coat pocket: a piece of coarse cloth the size of a carpet.

❏ **Item:** Left coat pocket: an enormous silver chest filled with dust that made us sneeze.

❏ **Item:** Right waistcoat pocket: a bundle of thin white stuff, each piece about the size of three men, tied with cable and covered in black markings. We think this is his writing.

❏ **Item:** Left waistcoat pocket: an implement with twenty long poles sticking out of it. We think the Man Mountain combs his hair with this.

❏ **Item:** Large right-hand trouser pocket: a hollow pillar of iron, about the length of a man, attached to a huge piece of wood with more strangely shaped pieces of iron sticking out of the side.

❏ **Item:** Large left-hand trouser pocket: another of same.

❏ **Item:** Small right-hand trouser pocket: several round flat pieces of red and silver metal.

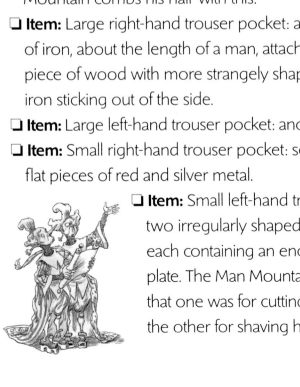

❏ **Item:** Small left-hand trouser pocket: two irregularly shaped black pillars, each containing an enormous steel plate. The Man Mountain explained that one was for cutting his meat, the other for shaving his beard.

In the top of his trousers were two tight pockets that we could not get into. He called them his fobs, and showed us what was in them.

In the right fob was a great silver chain, with a wonderful engine at one end, in the form of a globe, half silver and half transparent. On the transparent side were strange figures which we could not touch. The engine makes a noise like a watermill. We think it is either an unknown animal, or perhaps the Man Mountain's god. It is probably his god, as he told us he hardly ever did anything without consulting it first.

In the left fob was a net which contained several pieces of yellow metal. If these really are gold, they must be very valuable.

Around his waist was a great leather belt, from which hung a sword the length of five men and a pouch which contained several very heavy lumps of metal about the size of our heads and a heap of much smaller black grains.

Signed,

Clefren Frelock

Marsi Frelock

The emperor asked me to show him several of these things. He summoned three thousand soldiers to stand by, just to be on the safe side. I got out my sword, which flashed brightly in the sun, dazzling the soldiers and making them shout out in terror and surprise. Next I got out one of my pocket pistols and, putting some gunpowder in it, fired it into the air. As you might imagine, this terrified everyone even more than the sword, and hundreds of soldiers fell down in a dead faint. Even the emperor was badly shaken.

At the emperor's order, I put these and all the other objects that Clefren and Marsi Frelock had found onto the ground. My sword, pistols and gunpowder pouch were taken to the emperor's stores, but everything else was given back to me.

I did not tell the emperor that I had another secret pocket. In it I had a pair of spectacles, a pocket telescope and other personal items, which I was afraid might become lost or broken if I revealed them.

By being as gentle and friendly as possible, I hoped to be allowed my freedom. The people quickly lost all fear of me, often coming to dance on my hand. The children would even play hide-and-seek in my hair.

One day the emperor entertained me with a show that was the most spectacular I have ever seen. The most impressive event was the rope-dancing. This is a sport carried out by people trying to gain important positions at court. When a post is vacant, because someone has died or has been disgraced (which happens pretty often), the candidates dance on the rope. Whoever jumps the highest wins. Chief ministers also often rope-dance, to show that they can still do it. The treasurer, Flimnap, is allowed to dance on a very high rope. My friend Reldresal, principal secretary for private affairs, dances just a bit lower. Often people fall off the ropes, breaking limbs or even killing themselves. A year or two ago Flimnap fell and would certainly have broken his neck if one of the emperor's cushions had not luckily been there to break his fall.

I learnt that the emperor, empress and first minister sometimes hold a private competition in the chamber of state. The emperor or his first minister holds out a stick which the competitors have to creep under or leap over. Whoever does this the longest gets a blue piece of silk. The runner-up gets a red piece and the person who comes third a green one. All these are worn proudly at court.

I decided to organize some games of my own. I took some tree-trunks and my handkerchief and made a sort of arena on which twenty-four horses and their riders carried out lots of complicated manoeuvres, including fighting mock battles. It was

all very exciting. Unfortunately one of the horses put its foot through my handkerchief, throwing its rider. The rider was fine but the horse hurt its shoulder and I decided not to risk any more games like this.

A couple of days after this the emperor was inspecting his troops and decided that it would be amusing to have them march between my legs. There were three thousand soldiers on foot and a thousand on horseback. The soldiers were all forbidden from looking up – my trousers were in a very tattered state by now. Some of them sneaked a look though, and I distinctly heard their guffaws and titters.

At last my pleas for freedom were heard in the council. Only one person opposed it – the chief admiral, or galbet, whose name was Skyresh Bolgolam and who had decided that he was my enemy. Even he was finally persuaded: I had to swear an oath, and agree to obey the commands in the following proclamation:

"Golbasto Momaren Evlame Gurdilo Shefin Mully Ully Gue, most Mighty Emperor of Lilliput, Delight and Terror of the Universe, etc. etc., taller than the sons of men, etc. etc., proposeth to the Man Mountain that he shall:

- not leave our kingdom without permission;
- only enter the capital with our permission, and with two hours' warning to allow everyone to get out of his way;
- confine his walks to our main roads, and not lie down in any fields;
- be very careful not to squash people, horses or carriages when walking, and only pick someone up with their permission;
- if needed, carry a royal messenger across the country once a month;
- be our ally against our enemies on the island of Blefuscu and do his best to destroy their fleet, which is preparing to invade us;
- when at his leisure, help our workmen to build walls in the royal park and elsewhere;
- tell us how big our kingdom is by walking round the coast and counting his steps.

28

If he agrees to all this, he will be provided with enough food and drink each day to feed 1,728 of our subjects." (A friend at court explained that they had reached this figure by calculating that because I was twelve times taller than them, my body would contain twelve times twelve times twelve of theirs, and would need that times as much food to keep going.)

I of course agreed to all these conditions, although I wasn't totally happy with some of them (which had been added by my enemy Skyresh Bolgolam).

The first thing I did with my new-found freedom was tour the capital, Mildendo. I walked very carefully, in case anyone should still be outdoors. I couldn't reach the emperor's palace as the buildings of the court-yards around it were too high for me to step over, and I thought I might damage them if I climbed on them.

To overcome this I spent the next three days in the royal park outside the city, cutting down some of the largest trees. With these I made a pair of stools which I then used to step over the buildings. I lay down in the courtyard to look inside the royal apartments, which were magnificent. The empress was kind enough to hold her hand out of the window for me to kiss.

About a fortnight after I had been set free, Reldresal came to see me in private. He explained that all was not well in Lilliput. There were two groups at court, the Tramecksan and the Slamecksan, who hated each other. The Tramecksan wore high-heeled shoes, the Slamecksan low-heeled ones. The present emperor favoured the Slamecksan and wore lower heels than anyone else. His son, however, the heir to the throne, wore one heel  higher than the other (which made him hobble), indicating that he leant a little towards the Tramecksan.

The two groups were always plotting against each other. To make matters worse, the country had been at war for thirty-six months with the neighbouring country of Blefuscu. The cause of the war had been eggs.

Originally, everyone in Lilliput and Blefuscu had opened their eggs at the larger end. But the current emperor's grandfather had cut his finger as a boy  when breaking open an egg at the big end. Because of this his father, the emperor at the time, ordered everyone to open their eggs at the smaller end. The population resented this terribly; one emperor lost his life, and another  was deposed in the ensuing troubles. Eleven thousand people were thought to have been killed rather than agree to break their eggs at the smaller end.

Many others fled to Blefuscu. Big-endian books were banned and big-endians prevented from having jobs.

The emperor of Blefuscu even accused the Lilliputian emperor of creating a division in the religion, by going against the great Prophet Lustrog in the Brundrecal, their holy book. Lustrog stated that: "all true Believers shall break their Eggs at the convenient End". According to the Blefuscudian emperor (and all the other big-endians), this was obviously the large end.

The big-endian Lilliputians who had fled to Blefuscu finally persuaded the emperor there to wage war on Lilliput. So far the Lilliputians had lost thirty thousand soldiers and sailors in the war, along with forty large ships and countless smaller ones. Blefuscu had lost even more, but had managed to assemble a big fleet and was preparing to invade Lilliput.

The emperor had sent Reldresal to ask for my help. Although as a foreigner I felt I should not interfere in the arguments of the Lilliputians, I was prepared to defend the emperor and his country against invaders.

The island of Blefuscu lay around eight hundred metres off the north-east coast of Lilliput. No contact was allowed between the two islands and I had avoided that side of Lilliput, so that no Blefuscudian could have seen me, or had any idea that I existed.

I hatched a bold plan to capture their fleet. I asked for a large number of the strongest ropes and heaviest iron bars to be brought to me. The ropes were like thin string and the bars about as thick as knitting needles.

I twisted the bars together in threes and bent the ends to form hooks. I then tied lengths of rope, also twisted in three, to the hooks and, carrying these, set off for the channel separating Lilliput from Blefuscu. Just before high tide I waded out. I had to swim across the deeper middle part but within half an hour I was approaching Blefuscu. The enemy sailors were so frightened when they saw me that they all jumped into the water and swam for their lives. They then gathered in a great group back on shore; there must have been about thirty thousand of them.

Having reached the deserted ships, I started to fix a hook to each one, gathering the ropes attached to the hooks in a great bundle as I went along. The Blefuscudians tried to stop me by bombarding me with arrows, which stung terribly. My main fear was that they would hit me in the eyes and blind me. Then I remembered the pair of glasses hidden in my secret pocket. I fixed these firmly on my nose and was able to continue with my plan.

As soon as I had hooked up all the ships, I gave a great heave and ... nothing moved! The ships were still anchored fast, so I dropped the ropes and, getting out my knife, quickly cut through all the anchor chains. Then off I set back for Lilliput, pulling fifty of their largest ships behind me. When the Blefuscudians saw what I was doing, they let out a deafening scream of grief and despair. As soon as I was out of range, I stopped to pick out the arrows that had stuck into me,

and rubbed in some of the soothing ointment that had been given to me when I first arrived in Lilliput. I waited for the tide to drop a little and continued on.

The Lilliputians first saw the fleet approaching when it was in the middle of the channel. They could not see me because I was up to my neck in water. They were convinced that I had drowned and that the enemy was sailing over to attack them. They were about to despair, when they spotted me. They let out a great cry of triumph and as soon as I reached shore, the emperor made me a nardac, which is the highest honour in the country.

The emperor was overjoyed at the victory, and asked me to go back and capture the rest of the Blefuscudian ships. He decided that he wanted to conquer Blefuscu and turn it into a province of Lilliput. Everybody would be forced to break their eggs at the small end, and as far as he was concerned he would be emperor of the whole world. I tried to dissuade him from his plan, saying I didn't want to play any part in turning a brave people like the Blefuscudians into slaves.

Many government ministers agreed with me. However, the emperor never forgave me for opposing him, and, as I was soon to discover, began plotting against me with several of his ministers.

About three weeks after I had captured the ships, ambassadors arrived from Blefuscu with an offer of peace. I helped them a little in the negotiations, and when a peace treaty had finally been signed, the ambassadors paid me a visit. They invited me in turn to visit the emperor of Blefuscu.

During my next audience with the emperor of Lilliput I asked his permission to travel to Blefuscu. He agreed, but in a very cold way. I did not understand why the emperor was being so unfriendly, but I later learnt that Flimnap and Bolgolam had persuaded him that I had been plotting against him with the Blefuscudian ambassadors. I began to realize how treacherous courts and ministers could be.

About this time I had a chance to do a great favour for the emperor – at least I thought so at the time. One night I was woken by hundreds of people shouting at my door. Some court officials explained that the empress's rooms in the royal palace had caught fire. I rushed to the palace. The Lilliputians were already trying to put the fire out with buckets of water, but these were proving useless. I could have smothered the flames with my coat, but had left it in my house.

The fire was spreading and it looked as if the whole palace was going to burn to the ground, when suddenly I had an idea. That evening I had drunk a huge amount of a very tasty kind of wine called glimigrim, so I had a very full bladder. I quickly relieved myself in the direction of the empress's apartment and was able to put the fire out in three minutes.

Having done so, I immediately went back home. I knew it was strictly against the law for anyone to make water within the palace walls, but hoped the emperor would understand my reasons and forgive me. I heard that he did order the chief court to issue me with a pardon, but I never received it. What's more, the empress was apparently so disgusted with what I had done that she refused ever again to use the rooms where the fire had broken out. And she too began plotting against me.

Before I go on recounting my adventures, I should describe some of the more interesting things about the Lilliputians and their country.

They write diagonally on a page, from one corner to the opposite.

They bury their dead with their heads pointing downwards. They do this because they believe that in eleven thousand months all the dead will come back to life. At this time the earth, which they think is flat, will turn upside down, so that the dead will find themselves back on their feet. (Actually, highly educated Lilliputians think this is nonsense, but many other people still believe it.)

They think that deceiving people is a worse crime than stealing. Being ungrateful is punishable by death. If someone accuses another person of committing a crime against the government and the accused person is found innocent, the accuser is immediately put to death. The person accused is paid compensation from the property of the accuser and their innocence is proclaimed everywhere.

If anyone can prove that they have faithfully obeyed all the country's laws for a period of seventy-three months, they are rewarded with money from a special fund and are allowed to add the word snilpall, which means legal, to their name.

The Lilliputians' ideas about parents and children are very different from ours. They do not think that children should be grateful to their parents for having been born, and they think that parents are quite the worst people to educate their own children. Because of this, when they are twenty months old, all children except those of the poorest working people are sent to public nurseries or schools. There are separate schools for boys and girls, and for different classes of children.

Upper-class boys are sent to schools staffed by very distinguished teachers. The boys' food and clothes are very plain and simple. They are dressed by

The children are kept at school until they are fifteen years old (which is equivalent to our twenty-one), but are given more and more freedom in the last three years.

Middle-class boys have a similar upbringing, while working-class boys are sent out to learn a trade when they are seven.

Upper-class girls are treated very much like the boys, except that they are dressed by female servants, always in the presence of a teacher, until they are five years old, when they start to dress themselves. If any servant is ever found to have tried to entertain the girls by telling frightening or silly stories, she is publicly whipped, locked up in prison for a year and then banished to the most distant part of Lilliput. The girls' education is similar to that of the boys, except that their physical exercises are a little less strenuous and they are taught fewer subjects, although they are given lessons in how to run a home. They are considered old enough to get married when they are twelve years old, at which time they are taken away from the school by their parents or guardians. As with boys, working-class girls leave school at seven.

men until they are four years old, after which time they dress themselves, however important their family might be. They are always kept busy, except when they are eating and sleeping, and have two hours of physical exercise a day. They are brought up to be honourable, just, courageous, modest, merciful, religious and patriotic. They never talk to servants, and their parents are only allowed to see them twice a year, each time for only an hour and always with a teacher in attendance. The parents are allowed to kiss the child when they arrive and leave, but are not allowed to bring any presents, or speak fondly or whisper to them.

The care and education of the children is paid for by their parents. The poorest labourers, who tend the country's farms and grow crops, are not educated as children, but they are looked after in homes when they are old or ill. Because of this there is no begging in Lilliput.

I will now give a short account of my own life there.

Being good with my hands, I made a table and chair out of the largest trees in the royal park. Two hundred seamstresses were employed to make my shirts, bedlinen and tablecloths. Three hundred tailors made the rest of my clothes, and three hundred cooks, who lived with their families in huts around my house, prepared my food. I would put twenty waiters on the table to serve my meals, while a hundred more waited on the ground below. Their mutton wasn't quite as good as ours, but their beef was excellent.

One day the emperor decided that he and his family would like to come and dine with me. They sat on chairs on my table, with their guards standing in attendance. Flimnap the treasurer was there too, looking very sour. I ate more than usual, to impress the emperor. I learnt later that this had given Flimnap another chance to attack me, for he persuaded the emperor that looking after me was bankrupting the country. He said that I had already cost the treasury over one and a half million sprugs (their most valuable gold coin) and that the emperor should get rid of me as soon as possible.

While I am talking about the treasurer, I must take the chance to stamp out some evil gossip. It has been said that the treasurer's wife took something of a fancy to me, and even visited me alone, in secret. This is absolute nonsense.

She certainly came to visit quite often, but always with other people – usually her sister and daughter and a friend. But then many people would visit me. I used to put them in their coaches on a table with a rim around it. The coaches – often there would be as many as four at once – would drive in a circle while I chatted to the people riding in them.

Although Flimnap was finally persuaded that the stories were untrue, he continued to turn the emperor more and more against me.

About this time I had a secret visit from an important person in court. I had done him a great favour at a time when he had been very unpopular with the emperor, and I knew that I could trust him.

He told me that several powerful people had prepared a document accusing me of high treason. They were Skyresh Bolgolam, the admiral, who had always been my enemy and hated me even more after my victory over the Blefuscudians; Flimnap, the treasurer; Limtoc, the general; Lalcon, the chamberlain; and Balmuff, the chief judge.

The document accused me of committing many crimes, of which the following were the most important:

■ 1. I had relieved myself in the royal palace.
■ 2. Having captured the Blefuscudian fleet, I had refused to help the emperor conquer Blefuscu and turn it into a province of Lilliput.
■ 3. I had helped the Blefuscudian ambassadors.
■ 4. I had asked to visit Blefuscu, and, having only had spoken agreement from the emperor, intended to carry out the visit.

My informant told me that while the document was being discussed, the emperor had several times defended me, reminding the others of the various ways in which I had helped him. But the treasurer and the admiral would have none of it. They insisted that my house be set on fire at night, so that I burnt horribly to death, while the general was to send twenty thousand men to fire poisoned arrows into my face and hands. At the same time, servants were to be ordered to smear my shirts and sheets with a burning poison that would make me die in agony. The general was persuaded to agree with them, but the emperor still thought that my life should be spared. He asked Reldresal, my friend, for his

advice. Reldresal suggested that blinding me would be a severe enough punishment for my crimes.

Bolgolam, the admiral, was outraged. He accused me of being a secret big-ender, and maintained that this was quite enough reason for me to be killed.

The treasurer agreed, and pointed out that just blinding me would not solve the problem of the expense of keeping me. Indeed, I might eat even more when I was blind.

The emperor agreed that blinding me might not be a severe enough punishment, but he still didn't want to have me executed. At this point Reldresal suggested that I could be fed a smaller and smaller amount each day so that I would gradually weaken and eventually die of starvation. In that way, when I died there would be much less of me to rot and smell.

Everyone finally agreed to this, although the plan of starving me to death was to be kept a secret. The operation to blind me was to take place in three days' time.

Having heard all this I had to work out what to do. I thought of resisting – I could have easily smashed the capital city to pieces with rocks – but decided that this went against my honour as a nardac. Instead I decided to go to Blefuscu, as the emperor had given me permission to do.

The next morning I set off for the coast and seized a large man-of-war from the Lilliputian fleet. Taking off my clothes, I put these into the ship, along with my bedspread, and crossed the strait to the royal port of Blefuscu. The people there had been expecting my arrival for some time. They lent me two guides to show me the way to the capital, also called Blefuscu. The emperor and empress of Blefuscu came out of the city to greet me. I did not tell them of my disgrace, but said I had come to visit as I had promised I would, with the emperor of Lilliput's permission.

The emperor and his court treated me extremely well, although there was no building large enough to house me so I had a very uncomfortable time sleeping on the ground wrapped in my bedspread.

Three days after my arrival I was walking round the north-east coast of Blefuscu, when I spotted what seemed to be an overturned boat out at sea. I pulled off my shoes and stockings and waded out towards it. It was indeed a real boat, which was being driven to the shore by the tide. I immediately returned to the capital and asked the emperor to lend me twenty of the tallest ships he had left after the loss of his fleet, along with three thousand sailors. The ships sailed round the coast while I returned across the island. I stripped off and made for the boat. I tied the front of the boat to one of the Blefuscudian ships, and swam, pushing the boat with one hand and taking a lot of rests, until the water was shallow enough for me to stand in. I then attached ropes to nine more ships and

with these pulling and me pushing we got the boat close to shore. I waited for the tide to go out and then, with the help of two thousand men and many ropes and ingenious machines, managed to right the boat, which turned out to be quite undamaged.

I took ten days to make a pair of paddles and then rowed the boat round the island to the royal port. The people there were amazed at the sight of it. I explained to the emperor that this was a chance for me to return to my own country, and asked his permission to equip the boat and leave Blefuscu. He kindly agreed.

I had been expecting to hear something from the emperor of Lilliput by now. I later learnt that he had not realized I knew what he was planning to do to me, and thought I had simply gone to Blefuscu to pay a visit, and would soon return. I was away for such a long time that he became suspicious and sent an important person to Blefuscu with a copy of the document setting out my crimes. The person explained that I was fleeing from justice and if I did not return in two hours I would have the title of nardac taken away from me and would be declared a traitor. The emperor of Blefuscu would then be expected to tie me hand and foot and send me back to Lilliput.

The emperor of Blefuscu thought this over for three days and sent a message back to Lilliput saying that, although I had taken the Blefuscudian fleet, I had been very helpful to them when the peace treaty was being agreed. He could not therefore treat me like a criminal. However, he added, I had found an enormous boat, big enough to carry me away, so in a few weeks both empires would be rid of me.

The emperor of Blefuscu told me all this, and added in private that I would be protected by him if I were to stay and serve Blefuscu. I decided that I didn't really trust emperors and ministers very much any more, and said that, although this was very kind of him, I would prefer to try to get home. I gathered afterwards that the emperor and his ministers were all rather relieved at this.

I got the boat together as quickly as I could. Five hundred workmen made me a pair of sails, and the emperor's carpenters helped me make oars and masts. A month later I was ready to depart. The emperor and his family came to bid me goodbye. I lay down to kiss their hands and His Majesty presented me with his full-length portrait along with fifty purses each containing two hundred sprugs. I stored the carcasses of a hundred oxen and three hundred sheep on board, together with six live cows, two bulls, six ewes and two rams, as well as plenty of hay and corn. I would happily have taken a number of Blefuscudians, but the emperor wouldn't permit it. He had my pockets thoroughly searched and made me promise not to carry anyone off, even if they wished to go with me.

I set sail at 6 a.m. on 24 September 1701. That night I found a small uninhabited island, where I cast anchor. I woke two hours before sunrise and set off again, heading north-west. The day after, I saw a ship in the distance. I caught up with it that evening and found to my delight that it was an English merchant ship, returning home from Japan. The captain, Mr John Biddel of Deptford, was an excellent fellow and a very good sailor. Among the crew was an old friend of mine, Peter Williams, who assured the captain that I was trustworthy. The captain asked where I had come from and I explained as best I could. At first he thought me completely mad, but then I brought out my sheep and cattle, which convinced him that I was telling the truth. I showed him the portrait of the emperor of Blefuscu and some other souvenirs and gave him two of the purses of sprugs. I also promised him a pregnant cow and sheep once we arrived in England.

We reached England on 13 April 1702. The only misfortune on the voyage was the loss of one of my sheep, carried off by rats. The rest of the sheep and cows I put out to pasture on a bowling green at Greenwich. I made quite a lot of money while I remained in England by showing them to people, and just before I left the country again I sold them for six hundred pounds. They are doing very well, I gather.

I only stayed at home with my wife and family for two months, as I was desperate to see more foreign countries. I left fifteen hundred pounds with my wife, and found a good house for her in Redriff. My uncle John had left me some land near Epping, which earned about thirty pounds a year in rent. I also owned the lease of a pub, the Black Bull in Fetter Lane, which earned about the same. My son Johnny (named after his uncle) was doing very well at grammar school, and my daughter Betty (who is now married with children) was learning needlework.

On 20 June 1702 I went to the Downs and embarked on a ship, the *Adventure*, bound for Surat and commanded by a Cornishman, Captain John Nicholas. And so began my second voyage.

## A VOYAGE TO BROBDINGNAG

**W**e stopped off at the Cape of Good Hope. The captain fell ill, and we were forced to spend the winter ashore. We sailed east at the end of March, through the Straits of Madagascar and on into the Indian Ocean. On 19 April the wind started blowing hard from the west. It continued for the next twenty days, until we were well to the east of the Molucca Islands, when it suddenly dropped. I was very relieved, but the captain warned us to expect a storm, which duly arrived the next day.

The storm was terrible, and we were afraid the ship would capsize. We reefed the foresail and hauled aft the foresheet and did lots of other complicated nautical things. When the weather finally calmed down we found we had been blown so far to the east that no one on board had any idea where we were.

We were running seriously short of water by now. Luckily on 16 June the lookout spotted land. The next day we arrived at a large island or continent on the south side of which was a small neck of land jutting out into the sea, with a shallow creek next to it. We dropped anchor and the captain sent out a dozen men in a longboat to try to find fresh water. I asked if I could go with them.

We landed by the creek, but found no source of fresh water there. The men set off to search along the shore. I walked in the opposite direction, but finding nothing of interest turned to go back to the creek. I was shocked to see the men already in the boat. They were rowing for

their lives towards the ship, with a huge creature wading through the water after them. I did not wait to see what happened but turned and fled.

Pretty soon I found myself on top of a hill, from which I got a good view inland. Stretched out in front of me was farmland, with fields full of enormous grass, over three times as tall as I was. I set off on what seemed to me to be a major road, but which turned out to be a footpath through a barley field. The barley was ripe and about forty feet high, so I could see very little around me. After an hour or so I reached the edge of the field, where there was a massive hedge. Set into it was a stile into the next field, but this was much too tall for me to climb. I was trying to find a gap in the hedge, when I saw a giant just like the one that had chased the men in the boat.

Naturally I was terrified and ran into the barley to

hide. The giant came up to the stile and stopped at the top, turning to call out behind him. His voice was like thunder. Seven other monsters, who evidently worked for him, appeared. They carried scythes and began reaping the barley in the field I was in. I tried to keep away from them, but it was very hard squeezing between the stalks. I finally reached an area where the barley had been blown down, completely blocking my way. In despair I waited to meet my fate, convinced I would soon be squashed or scythed in half. I cursed myself for having ignored the pleas of my friends and relations and set off travelling again.

I could not help thinking of Lilliput, where I had been the most impressive thing the inhabitants had ever seen. Here I was as insignificant as a Lilliputian would appear to us. I even half expected to be gobbled up by the first giant who found me.

Pretty soon one of the reapers came right up to me. I was sure he was about to trample on me, or accidentally cut me in two, so I let out as loud a scream as I could. The creature stopped and looked around, puzzled. Then he spotted me and, bending down, gingerly picked me up between his thumb and forefinger, just as we would a weasel or other small dangerous animal. I was convinced he was about to dash me to the ground, but decided not to struggle. Instead I clasped my hands together and begged for mercy in as calm a voice as I could muster. His grip was so tight that I started to cry out in pain, pointing to my sides where he was pinching me. He seemed to understand and carefully put me in his coat flap. He then carried me over to show his master.

The farmer peered at me, lifting up my coat flaps with a straw. I think he thought they were a part of me. Calling the other giants, he put me carefully on the ground, on all fours. I immediately got up and began to walk around in circles, indicating that I didn't intend to run away. I took off my hat and bowed towards the farmer and then fell on my knees in front of him. I presented him with a purse of gold, which he peered carefully at and prodded with a pin. It was obvious he didn't understand its value, and he gestured that I should put it back in my pocket.

The farmer quickly decided that I must be an intelligent creature. He began speaking to me in his thunderous voice. I shouted back in several languages, but neither of us could understand the other. Eventually he got me to lie down in his handkerchief and carried me carefully home. He showed me to his wife, who screamed like English ladies do when they see a toad or a spider. She soon calmed down though, and afterwards became very fond of me.

It was dinner time, and the farmer and his family sat down to eat. I was put on the table, which was horribly high, and the farmer's wife minced up some meat and bread for me. I ate this with my knife and fork, which entertained the family enormously. I was then given a drink in one of their smallest cups, which was the size of a bucket. The liquid tasted like weak cider and was rather good. I took a great gulp, drinking to the health of the farmer's wife, which made everyone laugh uproariously. The master called me over; I found I was rather unsteady on my feet and tripped over a crust. Fortunately I was quite unhurt, although immediately afterwards, the farmer's youngest son, who was about ten years old, grabbed me by the legs and waved me in the air.

The farmer snatched me back and boxed the boy on the ear, ordering him to leave the table. But, fearing that the boy might hold a grudge against me, I fell on my knees and signalled that I thought he should be forgiven. The master relented and I kissed the boy on his hand.

In the middle of dinner the mistress's cat jumped into her lap. I was terrified at first and kept to the far end of the table. My master then placed me right next to the cat's head. The cat completely ignored me and I decided to be brave, for I had heard that running away from a fierce animal is a certain way to make it attack you. I therefore walked boldly backwards and forwards in front of the cat, which promptly drew back as if it were afraid of me.

We had nearly finished dinner when the nursemaid came in with a year-old baby in her arms. The child spotted me and immediately set up a deafening squall, demanding that I be given to him to play with.

The mother picked me up and put me in front of the baby, who grabbed me by the middle and put my head in his mouth. I roared so loudly that the brat got a fright and dropped me. I would surely have broken my neck if the mother hadn't caught me in her apron. The baby then started screaming again and would not quieten down until the nursemaid fed him.

After dinner my master went back to work. His wife, seeing that I was exhausted, put me on her own bed and covered me with a handkerchief. I slept for a couple of hours and dreamt that I was at home with

my wife and children, which made it all the worse when I woke up and found myself alone on a gigantic bed in the middle of an enormous room. I needed to relieve myself, and was wondering how to get down from the bed, when I spied two giant rats that had climbed up the bed curtains. The horrible creatures attacked me, but fortunately I was still wearing my sword and could defend myself. I felled one with a slash to its belly, and wounded the other in the back as it was running away.

Soon afterwards my mistress came back. She saw me all covered in blood and rushed to pick me up. I indicated that I was unhurt, and pointed to the dead rat, which she ordered the maid to throw out of the window with a pair of tongs.

My mistress had a daughter who was nine years old. She and her mother fitted up a baby's cradle for me as a bed. They put the cradle in a small drawer, which they placed on a hanging shelf to keep it away from the rats. The girl had very nimble fingers, and soon became expert at dressing and undressing me. She made me several sets of clothes of their finest linen, which was coarser than sackcloth. She also began to teach me the language, and gave me the name Grildrig, which means manikin or doll in English. I called her my Glumdalclitch, or little nurse. It was almost entirely thanks to her care that I survived in the country, and I will always be grateful to her.

Rumours of my existence began to spread through the area, and soon a neighbouring farmer, who was a particular friend of my master, came round to see

if there was any truth in the stories. I was put on a table in front of him, where I flourished my sword and greeted him in his own language, as my nurse had taught me. The man was amazed and advised my master to take me to the local town on market day and charge people money to see me.

Glumdalclitch was very upset when she found out, as she was sure I would be harmed or even accidentally killed by a careless member of the public. She had also realized how modest I was, and how ashamed I would be to be turned into a public spectacle, though I confess that I personally wasn't too worried by this.

The next market day I was put in a box, in which Glumdalclitch had placed one of her doll's quilts, and taken to town. Glumdalclitch came too, riding behind her father. The journey was only half an hour, but each step of the horse pitched my box about so much that I was terribly shaken by the time we arrived. My master took over a room at an inn and hired the town crier or grultrud to announce that a strange creature, about the size of a splacknuck but much cleverer, would soon be on show. A splacknuck is a graceful wild animal about six feet long, only found in Brobdingnag.

I was put on a table in the middle of the room and thirty people were allowed in at once to see me. I greeted the audience and drank their health from a thimble. I then flourished my sword and did exercises with a length of straw, which I used as a pikestaff. I had to repeat all this twelve times and was half dead with exhaustion by the end of the day. Fortunately no one was allowed to touch me except Glumdalclitch, although a schoolboy threw a hazelnut at me, which just missed. It was the size of a pumpkin and would certainly have dashed my brains in if it had hit me. I was pleased to see the boy well beaten and thrown out of the room.

My master announced he would show me again next market day and then carried me home. It took me three days to recover, and even then I had no peace, as my master insisted on showing me at home on every day except Wednesday (which is their Sunday). Realizing how much money he could make out of me, he decided to take me on a tour of all the most important cities in the kingdom.

And so around two months after my arrival, on 17 August 1703, we set off on a journey to the capital city, which lay about three thousand miles away. Glumdalclitch rode behind her father, carrying me on her lap in a box lined with quilted cloth and furnished with the doll's cradle. A house-boy rode after us with the luggage. The journey took ten weeks and I was shown in eighteen large towns, as well as in many villages and private homes.

On 26 October we arrived at the capital city, called Lorbrulgrud, which means Pride of the Universe. My master hired rooms in the main street and put up posters advertising me. I was put on show ten times a day. By now I could speak the language fairly well, and could even read some of it, having been taught by Glumdalclitch on our journey.

Unfortunately, the more money the farmer got from showing me, the greedier he became and the harder he made me work. The constant performing began to have a very bad effect on my health. I had lost my appetite and was rapidly wasting away. The farmer saw this, and decided to do his utmost to squeeze every last bit of money out of me before I died. Just at this time, however, a court official called a slardral arrived and ordered my master to bring me to the queen.

The queen was absolutely delighted with me. I fell on my knees and offered to kiss her foot, but she very graciously held out her little finger to me, which I clasped in both arms and kissed on the tip. She asked me a few questions, which I answered as best I could, and then invited me to live at court. I bowed low, and explained that I would be very happy to, but I was my master's slave, and so could not decide for myself. My master, thinking that I would soon die, agreed to sell me to the queen for a thousand pieces of gold. I then begged the queen to allow Glumdalclitch to stay with me and take care of me. The queen agreed and the farmer left. I could not bear to say goodbye to him, but merely made a slight bow.

The queen saw this and asked me why I had been so cold to the farmer. I said the only thing I had to be grateful to him for was that he had not bashed my brains out when he had first found me, a poor harmless creature, in his field. He had been well repaid for this by the huge amount of money he had made from me since then. I explained that the effort of entertaining the common people had been killing me, but I was sure that now I was under the protection of Her Majesty I would be well looked after.

The queen then picked me up in her own hand and carried me to the king, who was in his private rooms. His Majesty, who was a very serious person, did not at first see what the queen was carrying, and asked rather haughtily why she had suddenly become so fond of a splacknuck, which is what he took me to be. The queen then placed me on the king's writing desk and I gave him a short account of my story.

The king, who knew a lot about science, at first thought I was some ingenious clockwork toy, but he was thrown into confusion when he heard me speaking.

However, he refused to believe my account of how I had arrived in his kingdom and thought that this was a story concocted by Glumdalclitch and her father so that they could sell me for a high price. He summoned three very learned scholars, who examined me carefully. They decided that I could not be a normal creature, as I was too weak and puny to survive in the wild. I was much too small even to be a dwarf, as the queen's dwarf, the smallest one ever known, was still five times taller than I was. Finally they concluded that I was a freak of nature, or relplum scalcath in their language.

Having listened to all this, I then explained that I came from a country where there were millions of men and women just like me, and where the animals, trees and houses were all similarly small. The scholars refused to believe me. The king, who was wiser than the scholars, sent them away and called for the farmer, who fortunately had not yet left town. He interrogated him in private and began to believe that what I had told him might be true.

The queen ordered her craftsmen to make and furnish a splendid box for me to live in, and had clothes made for me out of their finest silk. Glumdalclitch was

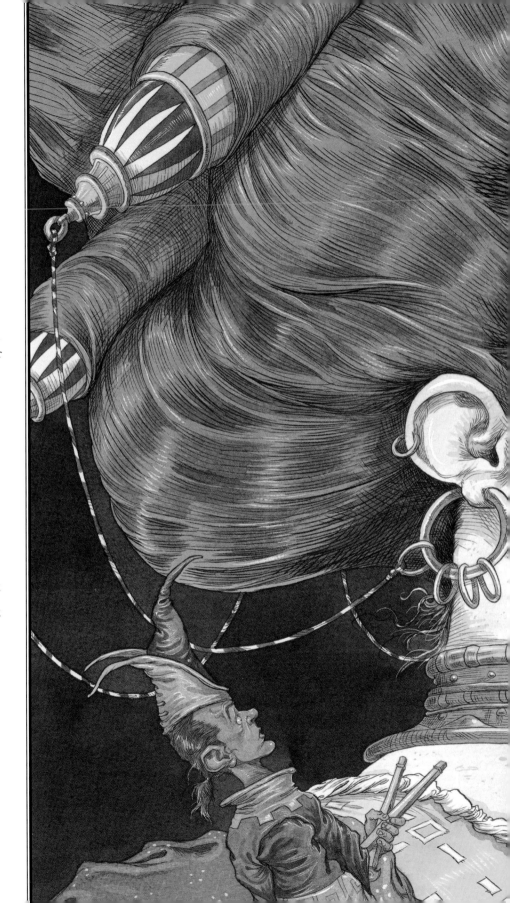

given a set of rooms and three servants; a governess was appointed to take care of her education.

The queen became so fond of my company that she insisted I always eat with her. I had a miniature set of cutlery which Glumdalclitch kept and cleaned herself. I admit that for a while watching the queen eat made me feel ill; she would crunch a lark's wing, bones and all, in her teeth, even though it was nine times as large as that of one of our turkeys, and would cram two huge loaves' worth of bread into her mouth at once.

From where I sat, her skin looked awful too. It made me think that the skin of our English ladies only looked so fair because we could not see it close up. I remembered that when I had been in Lilliput I'd thought that the Lilliputians had the finest complexions in the world. I had discussed this with a good friend of mine there, and he had said that in fact some of the ladies at court had rather bad skin, only I could not see them well enough. He also said that the first time he had seen the skin of my face close up, he had been quite disgusted, as it was all blotchy and filled with holes, and had horrible coarse stubble. And all this despite the fact that, if I say so myself, I am rather good-looking and fine-skinned for an Englishman.

Every Wednesday the whole royal family would eat together in the king's rooms. The king took great pleasure in talking to me and asked endless questions about the laws, governments, religions and habits of the people of Europe. He was always very wise in his comments. I confess I may have talked a little too much about the wars and political squabbles of my own beloved country.

Once he was so amused by my accounts that he picked me up and, laughing loudly, asked which political party I belonged to. He then turned to his chief minister and said how ridiculous human self-importance was when it could so easily be mimicked by a tiny creature such as I was. And yet, he went on, pointing at me, he was sure that back home these little creatures gave themselves grand titles and held elaborate ceremonies and thought their collections of nests and burrows as important as cities.

I was outraged to hear our glorious and magnificent country described so rudely, but then started wondering how insulted I really felt. I had spent so long amongst these people that I was now quite used to their giant size. I suspected that if at that moment I had seen a party of English lords and ladies in their finest clothes, strutting and bowing and prattling away to each other, I too would have found them quite absurd. I remembered the times I had stood with the queen in front of a mirror here and how ridiculously small I myself looked compared to her. I began to feel quite humble, and even to think that perhaps it was she who was normal-sized and I who had shrunk.

At court nothing angered me as much as the queen's dwarf, who, finally discovering a creature smaller than he was, behaved extremely rudely to me. Every time he saw me he would swagger past, looking as big as he could. I responded by insulting him, calling him brother and challenging him to wrestling matches. He played several tricks on me. Once, at the meal table, he wedged me into a hollow marrowbone on the queen's plate. It was beneath my dignity to cry out, so I was stuck looking very foolish for a good while before anyone noticed.

One day, he and I found ourselves near some dwarf apple trees. I insulted him unnecessarily, and in revenge he shook one of the trees, so that apples the size of beer barrels started raining down on me. I was bending over and one hit me squarely in the back. I was knocked flat on my face, but was otherwise unharmed. At my request the dwarf was excused, as I had provoked him in the first place.

Another time the dwarf became so annoyed at something I said that he dropped me into a bowl of cream and ran off. If I hadn't been a good swimmer I might have drowned, as Glumdalclitch was at the other end of the room and the queen was too shocked to do anything. As it was I swallowed a couple of pints of cream and had a good suit of clothes ruined, but was otherwise unharmed. The dwarf was thrashed soundly and made to drink the rest of the cream. Soon afterwards the queen gave him to one of the court ladies and I never saw him again.

The country I was in is called Brobdingnag. It is a peninsula, about six thousand miles long and three to five across. To the north-east there is an impassable range of volcanoes about thirty miles high. There are no seaports, as the parts of the coast where the rivers meet the sea are too rocky and the sea too rough. The country is therefore completely cut off from the rest of the world.

Brobdingnag is well populated, containing fifty-one cities, nearly a hundred walled towns and many villages. The capital, Lorbrulgrud, lies on a river and contains over eighty thousand houses. The king's palace consists of a group of buildings about seven miles in circumference. Glumdalclitch, her governess and I often used to go from here into the town in a coach.

On these trips I used a small travelling box, which the queen had asked to be made. It was square and had barred windows on three sides. On the fourth side were staples that could be fixed to a servant's belt. Inside, it was fitted with a hammock and some other furniture, securely screwed down.

I was very keen to see the tower of the main temple, which was said to be the tallest in the country. I admit I was a little disappointed, as it was only three thousand feet high, which I calculated was, relatively speaking, not much taller than the steeple of Salisbury Cathedral back in England. However, it was extremely elegant.

I could have lived happily enough in Brobdingnag if it had not been for the mishaps that kept taking place. One day when my box had been put on a windowsill for some fresh air I was attacked by about twenty wasps as large as partridges. I killed four of them and extracted their stings – they were about an inch and a half long and as sharp as needles. When I returned home I gave three of them to the Royal Society.

Glumdalclitch would often take me into the palace gardens, where I liked to walk about. Once I was caught in the open in a hailstorm and was so bruised that I had to stay in bed for ten days. A rather worse incident took place when Glumdalclitch left me for a while in what she thought was a safe spot. A spaniel which belonged to one of the chief gardeners found me and, picking me up in his mouth, took me to his master. Fortunately the dog had been so well trained that no harm at all came to me, though I was rather shocked. Glumdalclitch was very angry with the gardener, but the whole incident was kept quiet in case the queen became upset.

After this, Glumdalclitch became determined never to let me out of her sight. I had been afraid that this might happen, and had therefore not told her about several other events, such as when I had had to fend off a kite with my sword, or had fallen up to my neck in a molehill, or had broken my shin on a snail shell.

The queen made a lot of effort to distract me when I was homesick. She thought that I might enjoy rowing and had her carpenter build a boat for me (which I designed) and a wooden trough for me to row in.

Sometimes I put up a sail and the court ladies would use their fans to blow me backwards and forwards. I nearly had a nasty accident one day. Glumdalclitch's governess picked me up to put me in the boat, which was already in the trough, but I slipped through her fingers and fell. I would have died, if my clothes hadn't caught on a pin that was sticking out of the governess's waistband.

Another day a frog that had got into the trough when the water was replaced clambered into the boat and almost capsized it. It kept hopping over me, covering me in revolting slime. I thumped it with one of my oars, until it finally jumped overboard.

But the very worst thing that happened to me during my stay involved a monkey that belonged to one of the kitchen staff. I was in my large box in Glumdalclitch's private rooms. It was a very warm day, and the windows of my box and the room were all open. I was sitting quietly at my table, when I heard something jump in the window of the room. I looked out and saw a monkey the size of an elephant. It came over and started peering in the windows of my box. Spotting me, it reached in and grabbed me. It held me in one of its front paws as if I had been a doll, squeezing me painfully. The door of the room rattled and the monkey, startled, leapt out of the window and clambered up onto the roof, still holding me.

Glumdalclitch saw the monkey making its escape and let out a scream. The whole palace was in an uproar as people ran out to watch and servants rushed to find ladders. The monkey stopped on a roof ridge and tried to feed me, cramming some disgusting stuff from its cheeks into my mouth and patting me on the back when I would not swallow it. I think it thought I was a young one of its own kind. Lots of people laughed at this, although at the time I could not see the funny side.

Several men clambered onto the roof and the monkey, spotting them, dropped me and fled. I was sure I was about to fall to my death, when one of Glumdalclitch's footmen reached me and tucked me

in his pocket. I was so weak and bruised that I stayed in bed for a fortnight. The monkey was killed and people were banned from keeping any others in the palace in future.

All the royal family were very concerned at my mishap, but once I had recovered, the king teased me quite a lot about my adventure. I drew myself up and said that if I had had my wits about me I would have stabbed the monkey in the paw when it had first grabbed me, frightening it off. Everyone present laughed heartily and I realized that it was impossible for me to seem brave and important in front of creatures as grand as these.

And yet since I have returned home I have often seen equally insignificant creatures filled with self-importance and daring to puff themselves up and regard themselves as equals to the most distinguished people in the kingdom.

My daily mishaps and adventures, which Glumdal-clitch would relate to the queen, kept the court endlessly amused. One day we went out into the country. I was walking along and came to a cowpat in the middle of the path. Determined to show how athletic I was, I tried to jump over it, but fell short and landed in the middle, up to my knees. I waded out and had to be cleaned off by a footman. Naturally the story spread, and for many days there was considerable laughter at court at my expense.

I was often present when the king had his twice-weekly shave. Once, when my own comb was worn out, I asked the barber for some shavings from the king's beard. I fixed these into a piece of wood and made a very handy replacement comb. I also persuaded the queen's carpenter to make a pair of chair frames of the same size as the ones I had in my box. I wove together some of the queen's hair to make the backs and seats of these chairs and presented them to her. The queen asked me to sit on one of them, but I absolutely refused, saying that I could not possibly put the most dis-honourable part of my body on the precious hairs that had once adorned the royal head.

The king loved music and often attended concerts at court. At first I was taken to these, but the noise was so loud that I couldn't make out any tunes at all. Later, I found that if my box was placed as far away from the concert-room as possible, and I listened with the

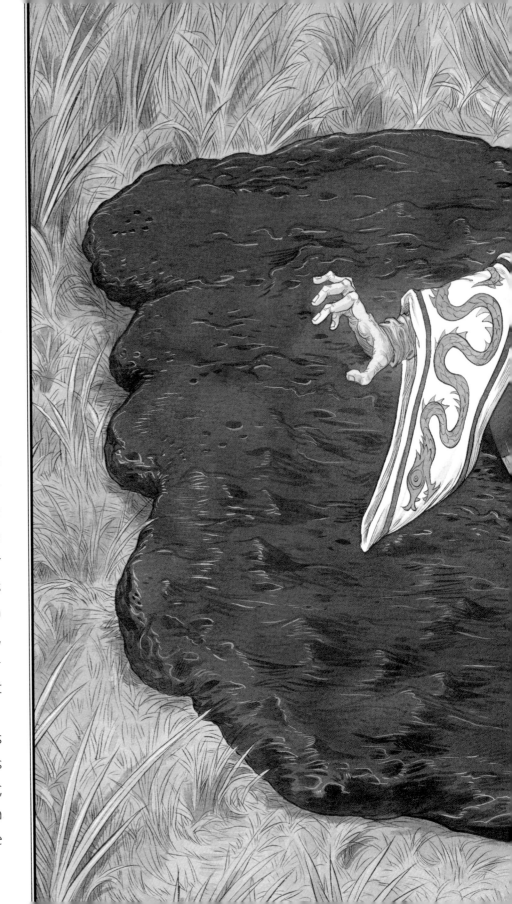

doors and windows shut and the curtains drawn, then the music sounded quite pleasant.

Glumdalclitch had a spinet in her rooms. I had learnt to play this instrument a little when I was young and thought I could entertain the king and queen by playing a tune on this one. However, it was far too big for me to reach more than five keys at once. So I got hold of two heavy sticks, which I covered with mouse skin, and had a bench placed just in front of the spinet keyboard. By running furiously up and down and hitting the keys with my sticks, I managed to thump out a reasonable jig. The king and queen were delighted, but I found it the most exhausting exercise I had ever undertaken.

The king and I spent a lot of time in conversation. One day I took him to task for always being so rude about the rest of the world. I pointed out that intelligence and wit did not always increase the bigger one was. Indeed, in our country the tallest people were often the most stupid. Amongst animals, bees and ants had a reputation for being far wiser and more hard-working than many larger kinds. The king agreed, and asked me for a detailed account of my own country, hoping to hear of some habits that his own country might like to adopt.

I began by explaining that our country consisted of two islands and three kingdoms, as well as colonies in America, all under one ruler. I described how the English parliament was made up of the House of Lords and the House of Commons. The House of Lords was filled with distinguished bishops and noblemen of the oldest and most aristocratic families, who were highly educated and always ready to spring to the defence of the kingdom. The House of Commons was filled with gentlemen picked for their great abilities and love of their country.

I then told of the law courts, which were presided over by wise old judges, and explained how well the country's money was managed, and how brave and successful our army and navy were. I worked out how big the population was by calculating how many members each political party and religious group had and adding them up. I finished by giving an account of our history over the past hundred years.

The king took many notes while I was explaining all this, and then proceeded to ask me lots of difficult questions. He wanted to know exactly how our aristocrats were educated, and how new members of the House of Lords were created if a noble family died out. He asked whether this was ever done on the whim of a prince, or by paying sums of money to a member of the court. He wanted to know how well the lords understood the laws of the land and whether they were so honest that they could never be bribed. He asked whether the bishops were always pure and holy, or whether they sometimes slavishly followed the opinions of some nobleman in whose pocket they were.

He then asked how people got a seat in the House

of Commons and whether you could be elected by spending a lot of money. He couldn't understand why people were so keen to get elected, as they were not paid any salary. He wondered whether perhaps they could make lots of money once they were members of parliament by taking bribes and generally behaving corruptly. He demanded to know whether in the law courts, lawyers were allowed to argue for causes that were obviously wrong or unfair, and whether belonging to a particular religion or political party could ever

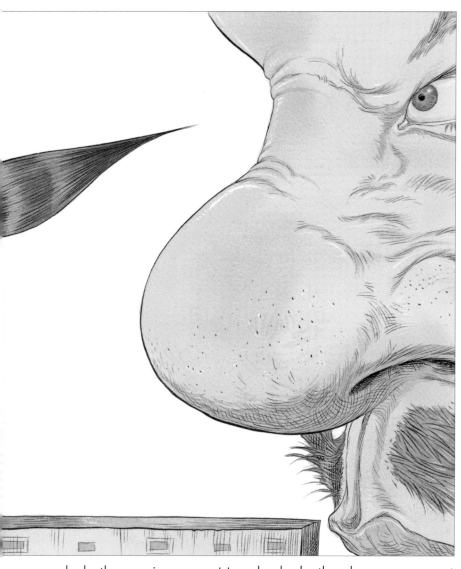

including greed, hate, dishonesty, cruelty, madness, envy and ambition.

When he had finished, the king took me gently in his hands and said that it was obvious from my description that I came from a terribly corrupt and rotten country. As I had spent much of my life travelling, he thought I might have escaped the worst influences of the place, but he had to conclude that the bulk of my country's natives were the most pernicious race of little odious vermin that nature ever suffered to crawl upon the surface of the earth.

I am very sorry to have to report this, but should point out that I had been as positive as possible in my description of my country.

Thinking that I might ingratiate myself further with the king, I started to tell him all about gunpowder and bullets and guns. I explained in great detail the damage these could cause and how he could easily make weapons that would destroy whole towns and kill thousands of people at once. I offered to show him how to do this, and how to make gunpowder, the recipe for which I knew.

The king was absolutely horrified by my descriptions and appalled by my suggestions. He was amazed that so powerless and grovelling an insect as I was could have such awful ideas, and could describe scenes of bloodshed and destruction so calmly. He thought the whole thing must have been invented by some evil genius who was the enemy of all mankind, and ordered me never to mention it again. I in turn was amazed that the king could refuse an offer which would have given him complete power over his subjects.

help them win a case. He asked whether lawyers ever at different times argued for and against the same cause, whether they were generally rich or poor, whether they got paid for pleading a case and whether they were allowed to become MPs.

He was completely astonished by the account of our recent history that I gave him, saying that it seemed to consist only of conspiracies, rebellions, murders, massacres, revolutions and banishments, and seemed to be the product of all the worst sins,

One day I told the king that in Europe there were thousands of books on how to run countries. He was appalled, and thought it meant we must be very stupid. He hated all mysteries and intrigues and maintained that you could govern using common sense, reason, justice and fair play. He stated that anyone who could make two ears of corn grow where one had grown before was more useful to his country than all the politicians put together.

I learnt that the people of Brobdingnag only study a few subjects, namely history, poetry, mathematics and morals. They are only interested in mathematics that is directly useful for farming and mechanical engineering. None of their laws may have more words in it than there are letters in their alphabet (twenty-two). Most are much shorter than this, and are set out in simple language that everyone can understand.

They have been printing books for hundreds of years, but have quite small libraries. The king's, which is thought to be the largest, only has a thousand books or so. The queen's cabinet-maker made a device on wheels that allowed me to read them, and even turn the pages.

The king's army is a militia made up of farmers and tradesmen, commanded by noblemen and gentlemen. It consists of one hundred and seventy-six thousand foot soldiers and thirty-two thousand cavalry. I often saw part of it exercising outside Lorbrulgrud. It was a truly spectacular sight. I had wondered why the country needed an army at all, until I discovered that there had been civil wars in the past, the last of which had been ended by the current king's grandfather. The militia is kept ready as a precaution.

I never gave up on the idea of returning home, although I had no idea how I would do this. The king had ordered watch to be kept at sea, and if any ship like the one I had arrived in appeared, it was to be brought with its crew and passengers to the capital. He wanted to get me a mate, so that we might have children. I could not bear the idea of producing offspring that would be treated like canaries in cages. Although I had been very well treated in Brobdingnag, I yearned to be home again, amongst people and creatures my own size.

When I had lived there for about two years, Glumdalclitch and I went with the king and queen on a trip to the south coast, where the king decided to stop for a few days near the city of Flanflasnic.

Glumdalclitch was quite ill there, and confined to her room. I was very tired and had a slight cold. I longed to see the sea and persuaded the king and queen to let a pageboy whom I was fond of carry me in my travelling box to the shore. Glumdalclitch was very unwilling to let me go, and burst into tears as if she knew something terrible would happen. The boy set me down among the rocks on the shore.

I felt unwell and, shutting myself securely in my box, lay down in my hammock. The boy must have wandered off, probably to look for birds' eggs. Suddenly the box lurched and I felt it being lifted high into the air.

I heard the flapping of wings above me, and decided that an eagle had carried off the box, intending to smash it open by dropping it onto some rocks. After a while there were several bangs and buffets and I felt myself falling fast. I landed with an enormous splash, from which I concluded that I had been dropped into the sea. I assumed that the eagle had been chased by one or two others and had been forced to drop its prize.

The box I was in was strengthened at the base by heavy iron bands and sat upright in the water. It was pretty watertight, apart from a small slit on the top to let in air. I was safe for the moment, but was trapped inside. I expected my box to be overturned or dashed to pieces by the first big wave that came along, or, if not, that I would die of cold or starvation in my prison.

After four hours or so, I felt the box being pulled along and started to have hopes that I might be rescued. Standing on a chair I yelled as loudly as I could through the slit in the roof. I then tied my handkerchief to a stick and thrust it out of the slit, waving it about frantically. I finally heard someone speak – in English! I replied that I myself was an Englishman who had suffered a terrible calamity. The voice replied that I was safe, as my box was securely tied to a ship.

The ship's carpenter was coming to let me out. I asked why one of the crew couldn't simply pick the box up and put it on deck. This caused much laughter.

I was finally freed and found myself surrounded by what I took to be pygmies, as I was so used to seeing giants. The captain of the ship, an honest Shropshireman named Thomas Wilcocks, took good care of me and made me rest in his bed. Before sleeping I described my box to him and said he should ask a crewman to bring it into his cabin. He looked at me as if I were mad.

The captain explained how they had found my box and rescued me. The crew had retrieved my belongings and taken some planks off the box to use in the ship. The rest had sunk to the bottom of the sea.

I asked whether any giant birds had been seen. One crewman had seen three eagles a great distance off, but had not noticed how big they were. The captain became rather suspicious of me as he heard me talk, and started to wonder if I might be a criminal who had been deliberately cast out to sea in the chest as a punishment.

Eventually I recounted my whole story. I was so convincing that the captain started to believe me. I asked that the small cabinet in which I kept my most precious possessions be brought to me. I showed him some of my treasures, including the comb I had made, along with another which used a nail clipping from the queen as its back. There were some giant needles and pins, the four wasp stings, some combings of the queen's hair and a gold ring the size of a collar that the queen had kindly given me one day. I offered this to the captain, but he politely refused it. The only present he would accept was a tooth that a dentist had taken out by mistake from a footman who had been suffering from toothache.

The captain asked why I shouted so loudly, and I explained that talking to the giants had been like talking to someone at the top of a church tower. I also told him that everything around me now – the sailors, the ship, the captain's cutlery – looked ridiculously small to me.

We had a good journey home and I arrived at the Downs on 3 June 1706, about nine months after my escape from Brobdingnag. The captain would not accept any payment for my passage. I borrowed five shillings from him and hired a horse and guide to make my way to Redriff, where my family was. Everyone I encountered on the journey seemed terribly small to me, and I began to think I was back in Lilliput. I was so afraid of trampling on people that I shouted at everyone to get out of my way, several times risking a beating for sounding so rude.

When I reached home I bent down to get in the door, for fear of hitting my head. My wife ran out to greet me and I stooped lower than her knees, thinking she would not be able to kiss me otherwise. Everybody looked like pygmies, and I told my wife that she and our daughter had not been eating enough as they were both shrunk almost to nothing. Like the captain, everyone started to think I was mad. I got used to being back after a little while though, and gradually returned to normal. My wife was determined that I shouldn't travel any more, but she could not stop me.

# A VOYAGE TO LAPUTA, BALNIBARBI, LUGGNAGG, GLUBBDUBDRIB AND JAPAN

**T**en days after my return home, Captain William Robinson, a Cornishman and commander of the *Hopewell*, whom I had served under before, came to my house. He was planning to sail to the East Indies in two months' time and offered me the position of ship's surgeon. The post was very well paid and I was able to persuade my wife to let me go.

We set off on 5 August 1706 and arrived at Fort St George in southern India on 11 April 1707. From there we went to Tonkin, where the captain had to stay for some time as many of the goods he had intended to buy were not ready. To help pay his expenses, he decided to carry out some local trade and so bought a smaller boat which he filled with goods. I was put in charge of the boat and given permission to sail among the nearby islands, trading as I went.

We were three days out when a storm arose. It blew us north-east for five days and then eastwards. On the tenth day of our journey we were overtaken by two pirate ships. Both sets of pirates boarded us at the same time. I ordered the crew to lie down on deck and we were all tied up.

One of the pirates was a Dutchman, who recognized us as Englishmen and swore we would all be thrown into the sea and drowned. I spoke to him in Dutch and begged his mercy, pointing out that our two countries were allies. He turned and spoke savagely about us in Japanese to his comrades. However, the Japanese pirate captain, who knew a little Dutch, said we would not be killed. He cast me adrift in a small canoe with oars and a sail and eight days' provisions.

Using my pocket telescope, I spotted several islands to the south-east and, hoisting my sail, reached the nearest in about three hours. It was all rocky. I managed to gather enough dry seaweed and heather to light a fire (I had a flint, steel, match and magnifying glass). I roasted some seabirds' eggs for my supper and slept pretty well under the shelter of a rock.

Over the next few days I made my way from island to island. On the fifth day I set off for the last of the islands, which was considerably further away than I had thought. I found a cave to spend the night in but was very unhappy as I could not imagine surviving for long in such an inhospitable place.

When I came out of my cave the next morning the sun was already high. Suddenly it was hidden from view by a huge object like a floating island moving through the sky. Taking out my pocket telescope I was amazed to be able to make out figures moving up and

down the sides of the object, along stairways and galleries. In the lowest gallery, people were fishing with long fishing rods.

Here was a chance of rescue! I furiously waved my cap and my handkerchief in the direction of the island, and began shouting out as loudly as I could. I saw a crowd gathering and pointing at me and then spotted four or five men running fast up the stairs to the top of the island. I assumed that they had gone to tell some important person about me.

The floating island came nearer and nearer and the crowd got bigger. I grovelled in front of the people watching, and begged to be rescued. One of the men then called out to me in a clear polite voice in what sounded like Italian. I replied in that language, but neither of us could understand the other. Eventually the people signalled to me to walk towards the shore. They moved overhead and let down a seat on chains. I got into the seat and was drawn up by pulleys.

I was immediately surrounded by people, all of whom looked amazed at me. I was equally amazed by them, for I had never seen such a peculiar lot. They wore extraordinary clothes and their heads were all cocked on one side or the other, with one eye turned upwards and the other inwards. In amongst them I saw several people dressed in what I took to be servants' clothes, each carrying a bladder that rattled noisily on the end of a stick. Now and then they would flap these bladders at the mouths and ears of the people standing near by. I later learnt that this was because the people on the floating island were always so preoccupied by thinking important thoughts that they could not speak or listen to anyone without first being tapped on the mouth or ear. The men with the bladders were a special kind of servant called a flapper (or climenole in their language) whose job it was to do this.

Flappers also attended people when they went on walks, as without being constantly flapped people were in danger of falling off precipices or walking into posts or knocking each other into the gutter. I was taken by a group of men up the island, towards the palace. I saw how necessary the flappers were as several times the people with me forgot what they were doing and wandered off, until they were reminded by their flappers. We arrived at the palace and were ushered into the king's presence. In front of him was a table covered in mathematical instruments. He was deep in thought and completely ignored us for at least an hour. Once he had sat back in his throne, pages flapped him gently on the mouth and right ear and he jumped, as if he had just been woken up. He saw me and evidently remembered that he had been told earlier of my arrival. He spoke to me, although I did not understand what he said, and a young man immediately came up and flapped me on the right ear. I indicated that I did not need this, which I later gathered made everyone think I was stupid.

I spoke to the king in all the languages I knew, but it became obvious that we did not understand each other. I was then taken to an apartment and given a splendid meal, with four gentlemen in attendance. The first course of the meal was all cut up into geometric shapes and the second course made to look like musical instruments.

I asked the names of many things during dinner, and the gentlemen took delight in answering me – with the help of their flappers, of course. After dinner a tutor with his flapper was sent to me, and together we began to compile a dictionary. I managed to learn several short sentences and over the course of the next few days, with the help of my excellent memory, managed to learn quite a lot of their language. I discovered that the floating island was called Laputa, although nobody could agree where this name came from.

The gentlemen who were looking after me, seeing how tattered my clothes were, ordered new ones to be made. The tailor arrived and measured my height using a quadrant, and then calculated my dimensions using a ruler and compasses. Six days later he brought a set of clothes, which fitted extremely badly as he had made a mistake in the calculations. Such mistakes were very common, and nobody commented on the clothes.

Meanwhile, the king had given orders that the island should move north-eastwards to a point over Lagado, the capital of the whole kingdom. The journey lasted four and a half days, during which I never once felt the island moving. On the second morning the king and his court played a concert on their musical instruments for three hours without an interval. The racket was awful.

On our way to Lagado, the king ordered that the island should stop over several towns and villages. Weighted strings were let down, to which the people below attached petitions, asking the king's favour in various matters. Sometimes gifts of food and wine were tied to the strings instead.

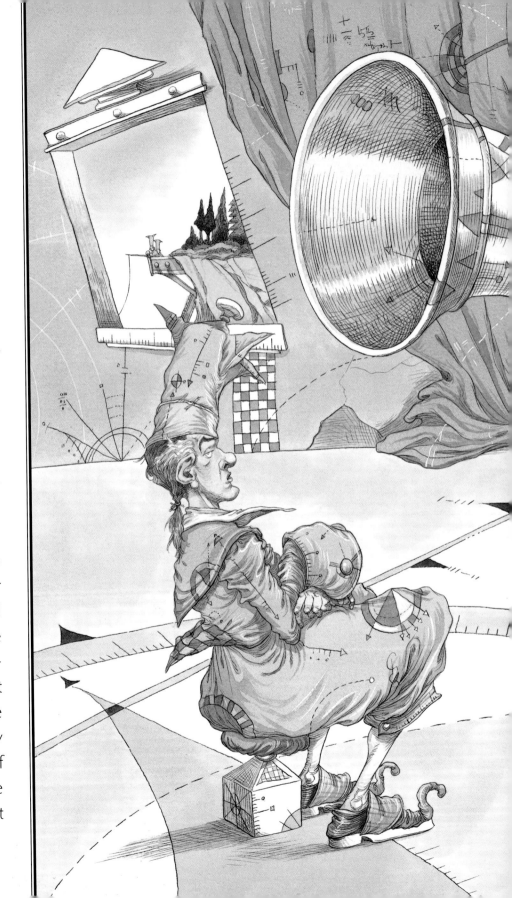

The houses of the Laputians are very badly built, with not a single right angle in any of them. This is because the Laputians cannot be bothered with practicalities, and the instructions they give their builders are too complicated for them to follow. The people are good at drawing geometrical figures and writing out mathematical equations, but are otherwise the clumsiest that I have ever seen. The only subjects they understand well are mathematics and music. Many of them believe in astrology and they spend a lot of time arguing about politics. I have found the same amongst many mathematicians in Europe.

They are in a constant state of worry as they believe that terrible things are about to happen to the earth. They are afraid that it is about to be swallowed up by the sun, or that the sun will become so encrusted with its own waste that it will stop providing light, or that it will soon burn out entirely. They think that the next comet which comes near (in thirty-one years' time, by their calculations) will set fire to us and reduce the earth to ashes. They are so concerned about all this that they cannot sleep well at night or enjoy the simple pleasures of life. Their first conversation every morning is about the health of the sun and the terrible dangers they face from the approaching comet.

The women of the island are very lively and have little time for their husbands. They are constantly surrounded by admirers who come up from the

country below. Their husbands are so preoccupied that, if their flappers are not present, the wives can carry on with their admirers right in front of them without their noticing.

Even though they live in great luxury, the wives and daughters hate being stuck on Laputa (which I personally think is one of the most pleasant places I have ever visited). They long to visit the capital city and see the rest of the kingdom below. However, they are only allowed down from the island if they can obtain a special licence from the king.

After I had been on Laputa for about a month, I had an audience with the king. He only asked about the state of mathematics in my country and was not remotely interested in anything else. He did not seem at all impressed by my answers.

The flying or floating island is circular and about four and a half miles across. The bottom is a thick plate of adamant above which are layers of rocks and soil. The top of the island is saucer-shaped, so that the rain which falls on the island flows in small streams towards the centre, where it gathers in four large basins. The king can control the amount of rain that falls by raising the island above the clouds if he wishes. At the island's centre is a chasm which descends into a large underground chamber called Flandona Gagnole, or the Astronomer's Cave. In this there is a huge lodestone or magnet which sits on an axle, enclosed by a cylinder of adamant. One end of the lodestone is attracted to a mineral found in the island below and in the surrounding sea, while the other end is repelled by this mineral. When the end that is repelled is pointed downwards, the island rises. If the stone is turned the other way up, so that the attracting end points down, the island moves downwards. If the stone is pointed at an angle, the island moves along as well as up or down. In this way it can be moved about over the land below. The island cannot move very far from the area where I encountered it as this is the only place where the mineral is found.

The lodestone is under the care of some astronomers, who follow the king's orders. When not steering the island, they spend their time stargazing. Their telescopes are much better than ours, and they have named many more stars than we have. They have discovered that there are two satellites around Mars, and have recorded ninety-three different comets.

The king uses the floating island to maintain control of his kingdom. If any town starts to rebel, he can keep the island hovering above the place, depriving it of rain and sunshine until they give in. If they still refuse 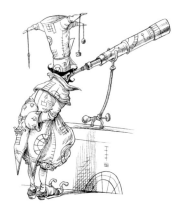 to obey his orders, he can have huge stones dropped from the island. As a last resort, he can drop the whole island onto a town, completely destroying it and killing all the inhabitants. He is very reluctant to do this, however, partly because he does not want to make his people hate him, but also because he is afraid of damaging the bottom of the island.

About three years before my arrival an extraordinary incident nearly destroyed the king's power. He had just been visiting Lindalino, the second most important city in the kingdom. Three days after he left, the city's inhabitants, who had many complaints about him, seized the city's governor and quickly built four large, strong towers, one at each corner of the city. The towers were the same height as a pointed rock that stood in the centre of the city. In each tower and on top of the rock they fixed a large lodestone.

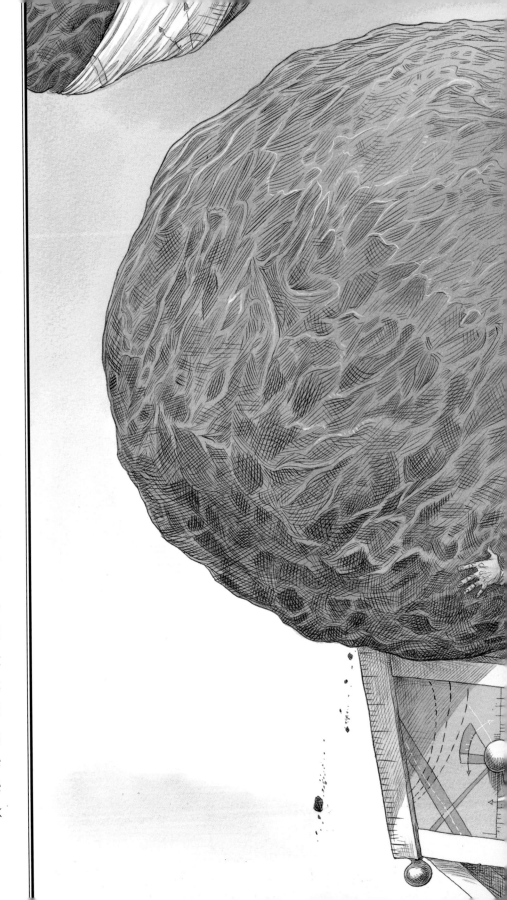

The king heard of the rebellion eight months later. He ordered the floating island to hover over Lindalino for several days to blot out the sun and rain. When this had no effect on the inhabitants, he had rocks dropped on the town. This did not work either, as the townspeople had taken refuge in the towers and in underground rooms. Finally, he ordered the island to descend slowly until it was just above the town. To the surprise of the astronomers operating the lodestone, as they descended, the island started falling faster and faster. They became alarmed and asked permission

to raise the island again, which proved very difficult. One of them then performed some experiments with small pieces of adamant and worked out that there were lodestones hidden in the towers and on the rock which were pulling the island downwards. The inhabitants of Lindalino had intended to pull the island down, kill the king and all his servants and change the government completely. Realizing this, the king gave in to the demands of the people. And now neither the king nor his two eldest sons are ever allowed to leave Laputa, and the queen is only allowed to leave once she is old.

Although I was not badly treated on the island, I felt neglected. The important men only cared about music and mathematics, and were not interested in my opinions on either of these. During my two-month stay there, I only managed to have sensible conversations with women, tradesmen, flappers and pages. There was one exception, an important lord at court who was related to the king. He was a very honest and honourable man, who had done many very useful things for the king, but all the court thought he was the most stupid person they knew, as he had no ear for music and was no good at mathematics. He often used to visit me, and wanted to know all about Europe and the other regions I had visited. He listened carefully and never needed his flappers when he was with me, although he kept two for when he was at court.

I begged this man to ask the king for permission for me to leave the floating island and visit the land below, which was called Balnibarbi. The king granted this, and he and my friend made me a present of some money. My friend also gave me a letter of introduction to a friend of his, Lord Munodi, who lived in Lagado. On 16 February I was let down on a mountain a short distance from Lagado. It was quite a relief to find myself on firm ground again. I soon found Lord Munodi's address. He was very hospitable and insisted that I stay in his house.

The next day he took me on a tour of Lagado, a town about half the size of London. It was a strange sight. The houses were very odd and many of them needed repairing. The people in the streets were mostly dressed in rags and were all walking fast, with wild expressions on their faces. We went out of town

into the surrounding countryside. There were people working in the fields, but I could not see what they were doing, and there seemed to be no crops or grass growing, although the soil looked very good.

When I made comments about the state of the country and its people, Lord Munodi told me that I should wait until I had been there longer before judging them. He then suggested that we visit his country estate, where we could discuss these things more easily. We set off on our trip, passing through more ruined countryside until, about three hours' journey from Lagado, the scenery changed. Suddenly we were surrounded by

beautifully kept farmland, with flourishing vineyards and cornfields and neat farmhouses. This was the start of Lord Munodi's estate. We reached his house, which was a splendid building surrounded by tasteful gardens with fountains and tree-lined avenues. I praised all this, but the lord did not respond until after supper, when we found ourselves alone.

He became very gloomy and told me that he was sure he would soon have to pull down his houses here and in Lagado and rebuild them following the latest fashion. Similarly he would have to destroy all his orchards and vineyards and start farming in the same

way that everyone else did. If not he would be accused of being excessively proud, ignorant and difficult, and would probably make the king his enemy.

He explained how this state of affairs had arisen. About forty years earlier a number of people had gone up to Laputa and stayed there for about five months. When they returned they were filled with all sorts of high-flown ideas, and decided that everything on Balnibarbi had to be done in a new way. They had got permission from the king to create an Academy of Projectors in Lagado where professors worked on new inventions. The idea had been so popular that there were now academies in all the main towns of Balnibarbi.

The academies came up with strange new ways of doing everything, including farming and building. The problem was that none of these ideas worked. Instead of going back to the old ways, the professors then invented even odder ways of doing things. Meanwhile, the houses were all in ruins and the people without food or clothes. Only Lord Munodi and a few others insisted on sticking to the traditional ways of doing things. They were regarded as ignorant and lazy and generally going against the common good.

On our return to Lagado, Lord Munodi arranged for me to visit the Academy there. I was very keen to see it, having been something of an inventor in my younger days. The Academy occupies several houses on both sides of a street and has, I believe, at least five hundred rooms all together.

In the first room I visited was a shabby bearded man whose hair and clothes were all ragged and singed. He had spent the past eight years trying to extract sunbeams out of cucumbers. The sunbeams were to be sealed in jars and released to warm the air during bad summers. He was sure that in another eight years he would succeed in his project. However, he desperately needed more money for his work, as cucumbers had been very expensive this year. I gave him a small gift. Lord Munodi had warned me that everyone in the Academy would ask me for money, and had given me some for this purpose.

I went into another room, but tried to turn back as the stench was awful. My guide persuaded me to go on, and warned me not even to hold my hand over

my nose as this would upset the experimenter. The man in this room was the oldest member of the Academy and his project was to try to turn human excrement back into food. The society made him an allowance of a barrel of excrement each week for his work. I saw another man trying to turn ice into gunpowder and a man who had come up with a new way of building, starting with the roof and working downwards.

There was a painter who was born blind and who had blind assistants. He thought you could work out which colour was which by smell and feel, and was

teaching his assistants to mix his colours for him in this way. Unfortunately the assistants still evidently had quite a lot to learn, and the painter himself made lots of mistakes.

In one room I met a man who had come up with a way of ploughing without a plough. His method was to bury acorns, chestnuts and other nuts in a field and then let in a large number of pigs. The pigs would root up the ground looking for the nuts, while also fertilizing it with their dung. He had tried out the method, and found it very expensive and troublesome, but was convinced it could be improved.

I found another room completely hung with cobwebs. The experimenter here explained that he thought spiders would be much better creatures for producing silk than silkworms. He intended to make coloured silk by feeding the spiders with coloured flies and thereby save the expense of having to use dyes.

While at the Academy I got a stomach ache and was taken to a room where a famous doctor carried out experiments to cure wind. He had a pair of bellows with a long muzzle attached. The muzzle was stuck up the patient's bottom and the bellows used to draw out the wind. If this did not work, the doctor pumped air in instead. When the muzzle was removed, the air came rushing out and carried with it the unpleasant substances causing the wind. The doctor demonstrated this on a dog. The first part seemed to have no effect, but when the doctor pumped air in, the dog swelled up fit to burst. When the muzzle was removed, the air that came out was truly disgusting and the dog promptly died on the spot. We left the doctor trying to revive it in the same way that had caused its death.

I will not tell you about the other experimenters I visited, except for one whom they called the universal artist. He had spent thirty years thinking of ways to improve human life, and had fifty men working for him. Some were turning air into dry, solid matter. Others were softening marble to be used as pillows and pincushions, and yet more others were trying to turn the hooves of living horses into stone so that they would no longer be able to be damaged. The artist himself was carrying out a new experiment to produce a breed of naked sheep.

We crossed the street by means of a walkway to the other part of the Academy, which was concerned with teaching.

The first professor I saw was in a very large room, with about forty pupils. He explained that he had come up with a wonderful machine that would let people write books on any subject without having to know or understand anything. It was a big frame in which were set many wooden cubes arranged in rows. Paper was pasted on each face of every cube with all the words of their language written in order. All the cubes could be turned, using handles that were fixed to the frame, so that the words on the uppermost face of each cube changed. The professor got his pupils to turn the handles and then made them read out the words softly

I assured the professor that if I was ever lucky enough to go home I would tell everyone there of his great invention.

I next came across three professors who were discussing ways of improving the country's language. The first project was to shorten all long words, and get rid of all words that were not nouns, to make conversations quicker. The second project was to get rid of words altogether. Instead, people would carry around examples of all the things they wished to discuss. A person could then simply show someone else the thing in question rather than having to go to the trouble of speaking its name. Not only would this speed up conversations, it would also mean that people would not have to learn foreign languages when they went abroad.

Unfortunately, women and common people had threatened to revolt if they were prevented from speaking their native language and so the idea had never completely caught on. Nevertheless, some of the most learned gentlemen in the country insisted on using the system. The only problem was that if they had many different matters to discuss, they would end up staggering under the weight of all the things they needed with them, unless they could afford one or two strong servants to help them carry them.

on the uppermost surface of each cube, moving along the rows. Each time they found three or four words that together formed part of a sentence, these were written down. The handles were then turned again and the process was repeated. The pupils worked for six hours a day on this, and the professor showed me several large books they had filled with bits of sentences. He intended to piece these together, to provide an encyclopaedia of all the arts and sciences. He was sure the work would be greatly improved if he could raise the money to build and operate five hundred such machines in Lagado.

In the mathematics school I came across a very strange way of teaching maths. Equations were written in non-poisonous ink on an edible wafer, which was then swallowed by the pupil, who was then only allowed to eat bread and water for the next three days. As the wafer was digested, the ink was supposed to carry the equations into the pupil's brain. Unfortunately this method wasn't working so far, because they had not yet got the formula for the ink right, and because the wafer was so disgusting that the pupils usually tried to sick it up straight away.

Quite the maddest people I met in the Academy were those who studied politics. Their ideas were so strange that I felt quite sorry for them. They actually thought that the best way to govern a country was to appoint people in charge who were honest, wise and clever, and who would try to do their best for everybody, not just look after themselves! They clearly had no idea about the real world at all.

There was a doctor amongst them who had several ideas for improving the way governments were run. He maintained that many of the bad habits of governments could be cured by treating them as if they were diseases of the human body. He proposed that every time a parliament met, doctors should be in attendance. From the way that the members of parliament behaved, the doctors could work out what was wrong with the government. They would then give out their remedies, such as tranquillizers,

laxatives, indigestion tablets and cures for headaches, and watch how the parliament behaved, changing their treatments according to what they saw. This seems like a splendid idea to me.

This doctor had also noticed that important ministers in governments seem to forget very quickly things they have promised. He proposed that anyone who had business with such a minister should finish the meeting by tweaking the minister's nose, or kicking him in the stomach, or pulling his ears, or treading on his toes, or sticking a pin in his bottom, or pinching him black and blue, to make sure he remembered what had been discussed. He also thought that every time a politician delivered a speech in favour of something, he should be forced immediately afterwards to vote against it.

When political parties were violently opposed to each other, he suggested that each politician should have half his brain swapped with half the brain of a member of the opposing party. The two halves of the brain would then argue away inside each skull, and soon come to a reasonable agreement. I also heard it proposed that all important positions in government should be decided on by a lottery as then nobody could blame anybody else if they failed to get one.

Although I had found the Academy interesting, I grew tired of staying in Balnibarbi and began to think of returning home. I learnt that on the northern side of the country there was a seaport, Maldonada.

Many boats sailed from here to the island of Luggnagg, which was quite close to Japan. I decided this would be the best route homewards.

I hired two mules and a guide to show me the way, and said goodbye to my host, who gave me a generous present as I left. When I arrived in Maldonada I discovered that there would be no boats sailing to

Luggnagg for some time. A gentleman I met there suggested that I could fill the time by visiting Glubbdubdrib, a small island near by. He and a friend of his offered to go with me. Glubbdubdrib means, I think, Island of Sorcerers or Magicians. The island is quite small and governed by a tribe of magicians, the eldest of which is the prince or governor. He lives in a palace on a large estate surrounded by tall stone walls. His servants are rather unusual, for he has the power to summon up any dead person he chooses and make them serve him for twenty-four hours.

We arrived on Glubbdubdrib at about eleven in the morning and asked to pay a visit to the governor. He agreed and we were let through the palace gates.

The route to the governor's room was lined with rows of guards or servants, who were dressed in very strange costumes and had a look that made my flesh creep with horror. We bowed low before the governor, who invited us to sit down. He asked me to tell him about my travels and, to show that we would be treated informally, dismissed his servants with a turn of his finger. They all immediately vanished, like visions in a dream. I was terribly shocked, but His Highness assured me that I was not in any danger. My two companions, who had visited the palace before, were not in the least concerned by what had

happened. I began to relax, and gave the governor a short account of my various travels, although I kept looking over my shoulder at where the servants had been.

I was honoured to eat with the governor. A new set of ghosts waited on us and I noticed that I was less terrified than I had been in the morning. I stayed until sunset, but humbly refused an offer to spend the night in the palace. My two friends and I instead took lodgings at a private house in the nearby town and returned the next morning, as the governor had asked us to.

We passed ten days like this, and I soon became so used to the ghosts that after three or four days they did not startle me at all. His Highness then said that I should call up any dead person I wished and ask them questions. Because there was no advantage to telling lies once you were dead, I could be sure that all the ghosts would speak the truth. I first asked to see Alexander the Great, who appeared at the head of his army in the park outside the room. We talked a little, though I found it very hard to understand his Greek. He assured me that he had not been poisoned, but had died of a fever brought on by too much drinking. Next I saw Hannibal crossing the Alps. He told me that he had not used vinegar to break the rocks blocking his way. I saw Julius Caesar and Pompey with their troops, ready to fight each other. I asked for a Roman senate to appear in one room and a modern parliament in another. The senate seemed to be composed of noble heroes, while the modern parliament was full of pickpockets, highwaymen and bullies.

Caesar and Brutus came right up to us. They seemed to be very friendly with each other. Caesar said that it was quite right that he should have been killed, while Brutus appeared to me a very good man. I had many conversations with him and he told me that he kept company with five good friends: his ancestor Junius, Socrates, Epaminondas, Cato the Younger and Sir Thomas More.

I met many other dead people. The ones I summoned were mostly those who had helped destroy tyrants and dictators. I also called up Homer and Aristotle and introduced them to the ghosts of people who had written about them since. These two wise men were horrified at how badly they had been misunderstood. I asked Descartes and Gassendi to explain their philosophies to Aristotle. The great philosopher freely admitted the mistakes he had made in some of his own writings, but also said that Descartes and Gassendi were obviously wrong. He predicted that the theory of gravitation would soon be found to be wrong too, and said that all new scientific theories were based on passing fashion and none would last long.

My friends had to go away for a few days on business and I passed the time in seeing some of the recently dead. I called up some of the greatest families of Europe and was amazed to discover that many could count pickpockets, servants, gamblers and assorted scoundrels among their ancestors. I was horrified by what I found out about modern history. I discovered that writers of history had told terrible lies, making villains into heroes and heroes into villains. I found how many excellent men and women had been condemned to death by corrupt judges and ministers and how many bad men had been honoured with riches and fame. I also found out that many great victories and successes in history had actually been the result of happy accidents. Three different kings explained that the only time they had appointed just and wise ministers was by complete accident because having good men in government simply didn't work.

I sought out some of the people who had done great favours for kings and emperors. Virtually all of them had died in terrible poverty and disgrace. I discovered that this was not a new thing, as I met a Roman naval captain who had been treated terribly by the court of the Emperor Augustus, despite his heroic actions at the Battle of Actium.

I finally took leave of the Governor of Glubb-dubdrib and returned with my two friends to Maldonada, where two weeks later I boarded a ship for Luggnagg. The voyage took a month, and on 21 April 1709 we arrived outside the port of Clumegnig in the south-east of Luggnagg. We were guided into port by pilots.

I was closely questioned by the customs officer. I explained that I had been shipwrecked on the coast of Balnibarbi and was trying to get home by way of Japan. I pretended that I was a Dutchman as I knew that these were the only foreigners allowed in Japan. The officer said that I must be kept under guard until he had received orders from the royal court. I was given some rooms to stay in, with a sentry at the door. I was well treated and had access to a large garden to walk in. Several people came to see me out of curiosity. To help talk to them I hired as an interpreter a young man who had been on the ship with me. He was a native of Luggnagg but had lived in Maldonada for several years.

After a fortnight a summons from court arrived and we set off for the capital, called either Traldrag-dubb or Trildrogdrib (it is pronounced both ways, as far as I can remember). Following the local custom, before we arrived at court a message was sent ahead

asking the king permission for me to lick the dust before his footstool.

On the appointed day I was indeed made to crawl towards the throne on my stomach, licking the floor as I went. Everyone who met the king had to do the same thing. Fortunately, because I was a stranger the floor had been well cleaned. I gathered that this is very unusual and that sometimes, if the person to be admitted has enemies at court, dust is strewn about on purpose beforehand. I have seen an important lord reach the throne with his mouth so crammed with dust that he could not speak a word. Nor could he do anything about it, for it is a crime punishable by death to spit or wipe your mouth in the presence of the king.

Worse than this, if the king wants to get rid of a nobleman, he has the floor strewn with a poisonous brown powder which kills the person who has licked it up within a day. In his favour, the king does make sure that the floor is cleaned after each poisoning, although sometimes the cleaning is not very thorough and the next person to visit may die by accident.

To return to my own story, when I reached the throne, I raised myself to my knees and knocked my forehead seven times on the floor. I then said the following, which had been taught me the night before: "Ickpling gloffthrobb squutserumm blhiop mlashnalt zwin tnodbalkguffh slhiophad gurdlubh asht", which means "May your Celestial Majesty outlive the sun, eleven moons and a half". The king said something which I could not understand. Instead I replied, as I had been taught: "Fluft drin yalerick dwuldum prastrad mirplush", which translates as "My tongue is in the mouth of my friend", meaning that I asked permission to bring along my interpreter.

Using the interpreter we talked for an hour. The king was delighted with my company and ordered his bliffmarklub or high chamberlain to have some rooms prepared for me, and to provide me with money for my living expenses. I was at court for three months and the king asked me to stay longer, but I decided that I should return home to my wife and family.

The Luggnuggians are a polite and generous people, although rather haughty. With the help of my interpreter I had many interesting conversations with them. One day I was asked by someone if I had ever seen any of their struldbruggs, or immortals. I said that I hadn't, and asked him what he meant. He explained that, very rarely, a child was born with a round red spot over the left eyebrow, which was a certain indication that the child would never die. The spot got bigger and changed colour as the child grew up. By the time the struldbrugg was forty-five it was coal black and about the size of an English shilling. At this point it did not change any more.

There were only about eleven hundred struldbruggs in total, of which the youngest was a three-year-old girl. Any family could produce a struldbrugg, and the children of struldbruggs were mortal like everyone else.

My eyes lit up, and I expressed my delight that I had found a country where at least some of the people had conquered death. Surely these people, no longer living in fear of dying, and having had so long to learn everything of importance, would be the wisest and happiest I had ever met. I was a little surprised that I had not seen any at court, for I assumed that they would be the most useful advisers that a king could have.

The person I was talking to looked at me in an amused and rather pitying way. He then asked me what I would do if I were born a struldbrugg.

This was an easy question, as I had often thought about what I would do if I found I was going to live for ever. First, I would make sure that I became rich, which should take about two hundred years. Second, I would apply myself to learning as much as possible in all subjects. Third, I would carefully record everything of

interest that took place. In this way I would become a living treasury of knowledge and wisdom for the nation.

I would not marry after sixty, but would live in comfort (though not extravagantly), surrounded by a select group of other immortals and passing on my wisdom to younger men. We immortals would take pleasure in seeing empires rise and fall and watching the effects of nature as coastlines moved and immense rivers dried up. We would see great advances in science and be able to make important astronomical discoveries. Governments would seek our advice, and we would be able to stop them becoming corrupt and useless.

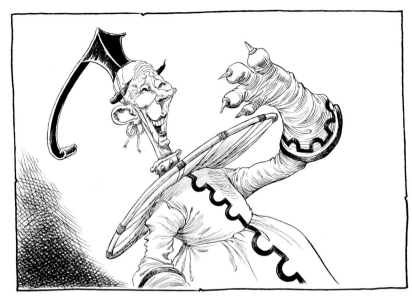

As I went on, I noticed that my friend and his companions were laughing more and more. Eventually my friend interrupted me. He said that, unlike people everywhere else in the world, the inhabitants of Luggnagg were not afraid of dying and did not want to go on living for as long as they possibly could. This was because they had the example of the struldbruggs to show them what it would really be like to live for ever.

My life as an immortal, as I had described it, would depend on my staying youthful, healthy and full of energy. In fact, the struldbruggs grew old like everyone else. Until the age of thirty or so they behaved much like normal people. After this they grew ever sadder and more depressed. When they reached eighty, they were as infirm and foolish as most old people, but the prospect of never dying made them even more unpleasant. They were bad-tempered, argumentative and greedy. They had no friends and no affection for their descendants.

They envied young people for being able to enjoy themselves, and normal old people for being able to die. The only things they remembered were those they had learnt when they were young, and they forgot many of these. Those who had completely lost their memories were the only ones who were remotely content.

If one struldbrugg marries another, the marriage is dissolved when the younger one reaches eighty years old. At this age they are considered legally dead and their heirs inherit their estates. After this, they are not allowed to work or buy land, or appear as witnesses in court cases. A small allowance is paid out of public money for them to live on.

At ninety struldbruggs lose their teeth and hair, and can no longer taste anything. They forget the names of things and people, and stop being able to read, because by the time they get to the end of a sentence they can no longer remember the beginning. In addition the language of the country is always gradually changing, so that the struldbruggs of one age cannot understand those of another. Those over two hundred years old cannot talk to normal mortals, and are like strangers in their own country.

I later saw five or six struldbruggs, the youngest of which was around two hundred years old. They were the most upsetting things I had ever set eyes on, and the women were more horrible than the men. None of them showed any interest in me at all, but they did ask for a slumskudask, or a token of remembrance, this being their polite way of begging, which they are not supposed to do.

Everyone in Luggnagg hates them and it is thought

to be a bad omen when one is born. Their dates of birth are carefully written down, although the records only go back a thousand years or so.

I told the king of my encounters with the struldbruggs. He teased me and said I should take a couple back to Europe with me, to help people overcome their fear of death. Unfortunately this is forbidden by law, otherwise I would gladly have done so.

I was determined to leave Luggnagg. The king agreed to let me go and gave me a letter of introduction to the emperor of Japan, along with four hundred and forty-four pieces of gold and a red diamond which I sold in England for eleven hundred pounds.

On 6 May 1709 I went to Glanguenstald, a royal port in the south-west of Luggnagg. From there I sailed to Japan. We landed at Xamoschi in the south-east of Japan, where I presented my letter. The town magistrates recognized the seal and received me graciously, providing me with carriages and servants. I travelled to Yedo, where I had an audience with the emperor. Through an interpreter I told him that I was a Dutch merchant who had been shipwrecked on a remote spot and had managed to make my way to Luggnagg. From there I had come to Japan in the hope of returning to Europe. I asked him to let me go to Nagasaki and the emperor agreed for the sake of his friend the king of Luggnagg.

On 9 June 1709 I reached Nagasaki after a difficult journey. There I fell in with some Dutch sailors off the *Amboyna*, a ship from Amsterdam. Theodorus Vangrult, the ship's captain, agreed to carry me for half the normal fare, on condition that I was prepared to act as ship's surgeon.

Our trip home was uneventful. We arrived in Amsterdam on 6 April 1710, having lost only three sailors through sickness and a fourth who fell overboard near the Gulf of Guinea. From Amsterdam I sailed to England and arrived at the Downs on 10 April, five years and six months after setting off. I went straight to Redriff that afternoon, where I found my wife and family well.

# A VOYAGE TO THE

# HOUYHNHNMS

**I** stayed at home happily for about five months but then accepted an offer to become captain of the *Adventure*, a merchant ship. I went to Portsmouth, leaving behind my pregnant wife, and set sail on 7 September 1710. On 14 September we landed at Tenerife in the Canary Islands, where we met a Captain Pocock, from Bristol, who was heading for the Bay of Campeche. I offered him advice on his voyage, but, although he was an honest man, I found he was a little too fond of his own opinions. I learnt later that his ship sank and everyone drowned except one cabin boy. If he had followed my advice I am sure he would now be safe at home with his family.

Several of my men died of sea fever and I had to recruit more in Barbados and the Leeward Islands. These new men turned out to be rogues, and convinced the rest of my crew to mutiny and take over the ship. I was taken prisoner one morning and bound hand and foot. I agreed to obey the crew and was untied and locked in my cabin, with one of my legs chained to the bed. The men told me they intended to become pirates. First they were going to sell all the goods on board and sail to Madagascar for more recruits.

I was kept prisoner for weeks. On 9 May 1711 James Welch, one of the men, came down and said the captain had ordered that I be put ashore at the first place we came to. He would not tell me who the captain was. The men put me in a rowing boat, in my best suit of clothes. They were polite enough not to search my pockets. I was allowed to carry some money and a small bundle of clothes but no weapons except for my sword.

They rowed me ashore and left me on a beach, telling me they had no idea where we were. I felt terrible but decided to go inland and bargain for my life with whatever natives I met, using some cheap bracelets and glass rings that I carried with me.

The countryside was full of grass, with fields of oats and irregular rows of trees. I made my way carefully, afraid that I might be ambushed at any minute. Eventually I found myself on an earth road, on which I could make out the tracks of many horses as well as some cows and a number of humans. After a while I spotted several animals in a field and hid behind a thicket to watch them. I must say, they were the most unpleasant creatures I have ever set eyes on. They had brown skins, long untidy hair, hooked claws on their front and back legs and no tail. They were very agile and often stood on their hind legs.

I was disgusted by the sight of these creatures and decided to continue on my way. I was walking down the track when suddenly one appeared in the middle of my path. He came right up to me, pulling faces as he did so. He then held up his front paw, although I could not tell whether he intended to attack me or was just curious. To be on the safe side I hit him hard with the flat of my sword. The creature let out a roar and a crowd of forty of the beasts came rushing up, howling and making horrible faces. They crowded around me, but I backed up against a tree-trunk and held them off by waving my sword. A few of them clambered into the branches and began dropping their excrement on me.

Suddenly they all turned and fled. I set off again and, looking around, saw a dapple-grey horse walking quietly through a field to my left. It was this that had made the creatures run off. The horse started when he saw me, but then recovered and came up to me, looking at me with wonderment. He walked around me several times. I tried to move off, but he calmly blocked my path. After a while I reached out to stroke his neck, talking in soothing tones. The horse looked a little disapproving and, raising his left forefoot, gently removed my hand. He then neighed in a way which sounded almost as if he were speaking.

Another horse, this one a bay, came up. The two tapped each other on the right forefoot and then began neighing to each other. They went off some distance and began walking to and fro, as if they were deep in conversation. They kept turning their eyes towards me, apparently checking that I would not try to escape. I was amazed to see ordinary animals behaving in this way and thought that if the country's inhabitants were as clever as their beasts, then they must be the wisest people on earth. With this thought I decided to go on and try to find a house or village. However, as soon as

I started walking, the dapple grey neighed at me in a very imperious way. I felt I could understand what he was telling me and turned back, waiting for any more orders. As you might imagine, I was not very happy about the situation I found myself in.

The two horses came up and examined me carefully. The grey one rubbed my hat with his right fore-hoof and bent it out of shape. I took it off to straighten it, at which both horses looked very surprised. The brown horse felt my coat flaps and again looked amazed. He touched my hand and seemed impressed by how soft and pale it was. He squeezed it rather hard and I cried out, after which they were much more careful. They both seemed very puzzled by my shoes and stockings.

Their behaviour was so extraordinary that I decided they must be magicians who had taken on the appearance of horses. I told them I was a poor abandoned Englishman who needed to be taken to a house or village, in return for which I would make them a present of a knife and

bracelet, which I showed them. The two horses then spoke to each other for some time. I heard them say the word Yahoo several times. I did not know what it meant but as soon as they were silent I said it out loud, imitating them as well as I could. They were very surprised. The grey repeated the word twice, as if trying to correct my accent. I tried to follow him, and found my pronunciation improving each time. He then said another word, which I can best write as Houyhnhnm. This was much harder to pronounce but after two or three tries I did quite well.

After more conversation, the brown horse left. The grey horse indicated that I should walk in front of him. Every time I slowed down he cried, "Hhuun, hhuun." I tried to show him that I was very tired and could not walk any faster, and he would stop to let me rest a while.

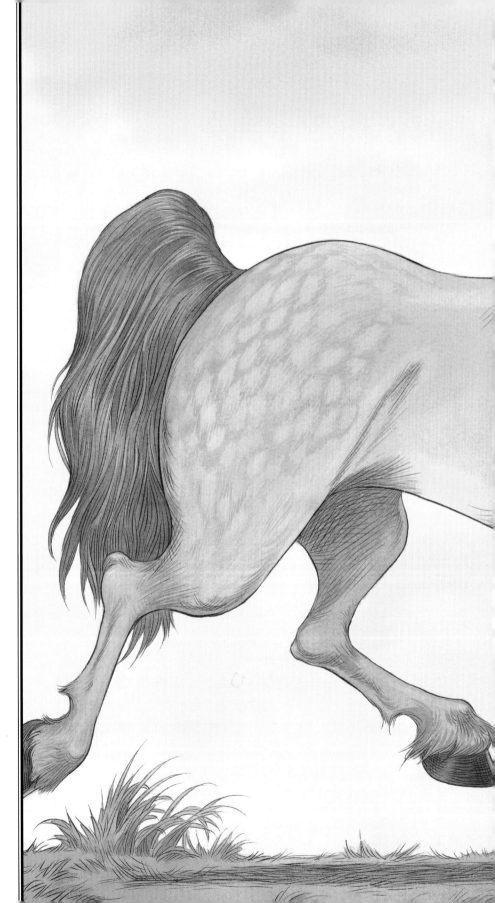

We eventually came to a long, low building made of timber with a straw roof. As we walked through it I kept expecting to meet the people who lived there, and got my presents ready to give them. But all I saw was horses. Some were sitting about on their haunches and others seemed to be acting as servants. I began to believe that I was dreaming.

In the third room was a very attractive mare with a colt and a foal, all sitting on their haunches on clean mats of straw. The mare came up and gave me a very uncomplimentary look. She turned to the grey horse and I heard them both repeat the word Yahoo. The grey horse then ushered me out of the house and into another building some distance away. There were three of the vile creatures I had seen earlier, tied by leashes to a post and feeding on roots and raw meat. The grey horse ordered a sorrel nag to untie the largest of these and lead it into the yard. I was made to stand next to it. To my horror and astonishment I realized that the creature had all the appearance of a human.

The horses obviously saw the similarities between us, but were confused by my clothes, as they had evidently never seen such things before. The sorrel nag then offered me a root which, as soon as I had smelt it, I returned as politely as I could. He then brought out a piece of donkey flesh from the Yahoo's kennel. This smelt so horrible that I turned away in disgust. He threw it to the Yahoo, which greedily ate it. Later he showed me some hay and oats, but I shook my head, to show that I could not eat these either. I was beginning to think that I would starve, when the grey horse put his hoof to his mouth and made other gestures that were obviously asking me what I wanted to eat. At this point a cow passed by and I mimicked milking her. The grey horse understood, and led me back to the house where there was a whole room full of milk stored in jars. I drank a bowlful and felt much better.

Around midday an old lame horse appeared at the house in a sledge drawn by four Yahoos. He had come to dine with the grey horse. The family ate in the best room and had oats boiled in milk for the main course. The old horse ate these warm, the rest cold. They all sat in a circle while eating, and the colt and foal behaved very well. The grey horse ordered me to stand next to the old horse, and the two of them evidently spent much of the meal talking about me.

I had happened to put on a pair of gloves, which puzzled the horses greatly. The grey horse touched them several times with his hoof and I took the gloves off and put them in a pocket, which much impressed the horses. I was ordered to speak the few words I knew and the grey horse then taught me the words for oats, milk, fire and water. I learnt these quickly, having always been very good at languages.

After dinner the master horse took me aside and indicated that he was worried that I had nothing to eat. I had thought about this, and this time asked for some hlunnh, or oats. I heated these on the fire, rubbed them and mixed them with water to make oatcakes, which I ate

with some milk. Although it was a very plain diet, I grew used to it and found it very healthy. During my whole stay in the country, I never suffered a moment's sickness. I did sometimes vary my diet with rabbits or birds caught with snares made of Yahoo hair, and collected herbs to eat as salads; I even sometimes found wild honey and occasionally made some butter. At first I craved salt, but after a while I didn't miss it at all.

I spent most of my time learning the language, which is full of high-pitched noises. My master, the grey horse, his children and his servants all thought it extraordinary that an animal such as I could learn to speak like a rational creature, and were very keen to teach me, so I learnt quickly.

My master spent a lot of time with me. He later told me that he was convinced I must be a Yahoo, but was astonished by my cleanliness and politeness, and by the fact that I could be taught. It was well known that Yahoos, with their mischief and cunning, were impossible to train. He was most puzzled by my clothes, which I never took off when any Houyhnhnms were around, and he often wondered whether they were a part of me or not.

After about three months, I knew the language well enough to be able to answer most of his questions. He wanted to know which part of the country I came from, and how I had been taught. I explained that I had come over the sea from a distant place, in a big hollow vessel made of the bodies of trees, and that my companions had forced me to land on this coast. He replied that this was impossible and that I must be mistaken, or that I had said the thing which was not (he meant lying, but the Houyhnhnms have no word for this).

I became better and better at speaking the language, and many Houyhnhnms in the neighbourhood came to visit and ask me questions. None of them could decide whether I was a Yahoo or not. My hands and feet were very like a Yahoo's, but my body looked very different, because of my clothes.

I had deliberately kept the secret of my clothes hidden. I loathed the Yahoos and I wanted to appear as different as possible from them. I was eventually found out, though. I used to take off my clothes at night and cover myself with them. One morning my master sent the sorrel nag to fetch me early. I was fast asleep and my clothes had fallen off me in the night. The nag saw my bare body and became very confused. He reported what he had seen to his master, who asked me to explain.

I told my master that where I came from we all covered our bodies with stuff made from animal hair, to protect ourselves from the weather and for the sake of decency. I would be happy to show him, as long as he excused me from exposing those parts which nature had taught us to keep hidden. My master was

very puzzled by my speech, especially the last part, as he could not understand why nature should teach us to hide anything that nature had given us. Neither he nor any of his kind were ashamed of any part of their bodies.

I then took off my clothes one by one, but kept my shirt on, wrapping it around my waist like a girdle. My master watched all this with fascination. He looked carefully at me and said that I was indeed a perfect Yahoo, but that I differed from all other Yahoos in several ways, particularly in the whiteness and softness of my skin, the shortness of my claws and my habit of always walking on my hind legs.

I was very upset that he kept referring to me as a Yahoo, as I had nothing but hatred and contempt for the vile animals. I begged him not to call me by the name any more, and to ask his family and friends to do likewise.

My master was very keen to hear everything I could tell him about myself, and I redoubled my efforts to learn the language. I repeated the story of my shipwreck, but he wanted to know who had built the ship, and could not believe that the Houyhnhnms of my country would leave a group of Yahoos in charge of such a thing.

I said I would explain, but he must first give me his word that he would not be offended by anything that I might tell him. I added that I had been astonished to find Houyhnhnms behaving as rational creatures in this country, and that if I were to recount my adventures on my return home, nobody would believe me, and would indeed think that I said the thing which was not.

My master was very troubled by this. Houyhnhnms believe that the purpose of talking is to make us understand each other, and so cannot understand why anybody should ever want to lie or why someone should disbelieve what another told them.

I told my master that Yahoos were in charge in my country. He was amazed, and asked whether there were any Houyhnhnms there – and if so what they did. I said there were many, and that they grazed in fields during the summer and were kept in houses in winter, when they were fed on hay and oats. Yahoo servants brushed their coats, combed their manes, picked their feet, made their beds and fed them. My master said this clearly showed that whatever the Yahoos thought, it was the Houyhnhnms who were in charge.

I went on to explain that Houyhnhnms were called horses in my country. When kept by upper-class people they were usually well looked after until they became ill or lame. They were then sold and worked hard until they died, after which their skins were stripped off and sold and their bodies left to be eaten by dogs. Horses kept by other kinds of people were less lucky. They were worked harder and fed worse. I told him how we rode, and described bits, spurs, saddles and harnesses. I explained that pieces of a hard substance called iron were fixed to our horses' hooves, to preserve them when they walked on roads.

My master couldn't understand how we dared ride on a Houyhnhnm, as even the weakest could throw one of us off, or roll over on us, crushing us to death. I described how our horses were broken in and said that most of our stallions were castrated to make them behave better.

It was hard to explain all this, as the Houyhnhnms have far fewer words than we do. Still, my master understood enough to be disgusted with my description of the way we treated our horses.

He then wanted to know whether the other Yahoos in my country were like me or more like the Yahoos that he knew. I said that they were like me, although the females had even softer and whiter skin. He pointed out that I was an even more feeble creature than his country's Yahoos. My claws were useless and my fore-feet were too weak to walk on. By insisting on walking on only two feet I was constantly at risk of falling over. I needed to protect my body against heat and cold, and my hind-feet from sharp stones.

He then asked about my own history. I briefly explained that I was a ship's surgeon, born of honest parents, who had travelled to gain riches to maintain myself and my family. On my last voyage, which had been a very hazardous one, I had had fifty Yahoos under me. Many of these had died at sea and I'd had to replace them. My master asked how I persuaded these replacements to join me in what was obviously a dangerous undertaking. I explained that they were all desperate people, forced to flee their homes because they were very poor or had committed crimes, such as treason, murder, robbery, forgery and desertion. None of them dared return to their native countries.

My master kept interrupting and asking what I meant by these crimes and why anyone would commit them. I tried to explain about the desire for power and riches, and the terrible effects of greed and envy. My master was constantly amazed at what I told him, but eventually he began to understand something of what humans in our part of the world were capable of. He then asked for a detailed account of the history of the region we call Europe.

Over the next two years I told him as much as I could about Europe and our arts, sciences and industry. I told him about our revolution under the Prince of Orange, and the long war with France in which I estimated that about a million Yahoos might have been killed, a hundred cities taken and five hundred ships burnt or sunk.

He asked me about the causes of wars, which I said were innumerable. Sometimes they were fought because of the ambitions of kings, who never thought they had enough land or people to rule over. Sometimes they were started by corrupt ministers to divert people's attention away from bad government. Differences of opinion had caused many, and the fiercest were invariably fought over the least important matters. If a king invaded a country where the people were poor and ignorant, it was perfectly all right for him to kill half of them and make slaves of the rest. It was also all right for him to turn on a king whom he had previously helped.

Because of the popularity of wars, the trade of the soldier, which was to kill in cold blood as many of

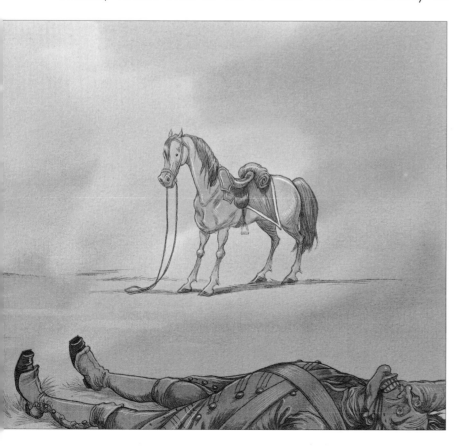

his own kind as possible, was considered the most honourable trade of all.

My master then said it was fortunate that we were such weak creatures. We could not easily bite each other, and our blunt claws could not do much damage. He could not see how we were able to kill each other in the numbers I had described and so thought I must have said the thing which was not.

I shook my head and gave him a long and bloody description of all the ways we had found of killing people, of muskets and cannons and bayonets, of sieges and sea battles and bombardments, of ships blown up with a thousand men on board and of dead bodies dropping in pieces from the skies.

My master stopped me here, and said that my description had made him loathe the whole race of Yahoos even more. Although he hated the Yahoos in his own country, he did not blame them for their habits any more than he blamed a gnnayh (a bird of prey) for its cruelty, or a sharp stone for cutting his hoof. But the Yahoos I described pretended to be reasonable creatures and yet behaved in a terrible way. He thought this was monstrous.

He then asked me to explain more about the law. He did not see the point of it, as he thought that reason and common sense were all that we should need to govern our actions. I said that I didn't know much, although I had hired lawyers to try to right some wrongs that had been done to me, without success. I explained that lawyers were a group of men brought up to be able to show that black was white and white black. Everyone was enslaved by these people.

As an example, I said, if I own a cow and my neighbour decides he wants it, he will hire a lawyer to say the cow is rightfully his. I have to hire another lawyer to defend myself. My lawyer is at a terrible disadvantage, as he has to try to defend the truth, which goes against everything he has ever been taught. I therefore have only two choices. The first is to bribe my opponent's lawyer so that he will deliberately lose his case. The second is for my lawyer to make my case seem as unjust as possible. If he does this well, we are bound to win.

My master said it was obvious that lawyers were clever creatures, and it was a shame that they did not spend their time teaching others. I said that they were in fact the most ignorant and stupid people, who despised all knowledge and learning.

I had mentioned hiring and my master asked what this meant. I therefore had to explain about money. I said that all Yahoos wanted to get rich so that they could buy great houses, fine clothes and expensive food and drink, and have their pick of the most beautiful Yahoo females. I told him that almost all the population lived miserably, and worked hard every day for tiny wages so that a few people could live in great luxury. My master could not understand this, as he assumed that all creatures had a right to their fair share of the things that nature produced. He then asked what all these luxuries that people desired were.

I told him as best I could, and explained that they came from all the far corners of the world. I said that you would need to go round the world three times before

you had gathered all the things that one of our better female Yahoos needed just for her breakfast.

My master said we must live in a miserable country, which had so little food and fresh water that we had to go overseas to get enough to eat and drink. I explained that actually my country produced three times as much food as it needed to feed all its people, and that very good drinks could be made from the fruits and grains that grew there. The main drink we imported was wine, which we drank not to satisfy our thirst, but to make us merry and forget our worries. It made us behave madly, lose the use of our legs and then fall into a deep sleep from which we awoke feeling sick and depressed. Drinking it filled us with diseases which made our lives uncomfortable and short.

I then tried to explain about doctors, who made their money attending to the sick, but my master found this very hard to understand. He said that Houyhnhnms grew weak a few days before they died, and occasionally hurt a limb, but otherwise were always healthy. I pointed out that my countrymen were continually eating when they were not hungry and drinking when they were not thirsty. They sat up all night drinking strong drinks on an empty stomach and they caught vile diseases from each other. Because of all this, they were plagued with hundreds of different sorts of illnesses. Doctors thought that the best way to treat these diseases was to give people laxatives or things to make them sick. The medicines they prescribed were made of all sorts of disgusting things.

As well as real diseases, there were many imaginary ones, for which the doctors had invented imaginary cures. In the case of real diseases, doctors could usually say confidently when a patient was going to die, but not when he or she would be cured. If they looked like getting it wrong, they could speed up the patient's end with some of their special medicines. These medicines were found especially useful by people who had grown tired of their mates, by sons impatient to inherit their parents' money, and by kings and chief ministers.

It is true that I might be sounding a little harsh on my own kind, but I was so impressed by the Houyhnhnms that I could not think of telling lies. In addition, the more time I spent with my master, the more terrible human behaviour seemed to me. In fact, I had been in the country less than a year when I decided that I wanted to spend the rest of my life there.

One day my master asked me to sit down near him (the first time he had done me this honour), and said he had been thinking about what I had told him. He was sure that I and my kind were a form of Yahoo, physically weaker than the normal sort but with a small amount of intelligence. Not only did I look almost identical to a Yahoo, but many of the things Yahoos did were similar to the ways that I had described my countrymen as behaving.

Groups of Yahoos were always having fights for no reason that anyone could see. He told me that in some of the country's fields there were shiny stones that the Yahoos were violently fond of. They would spend days digging them out of the ground and carrying them back to their kennels, where they buried them, looking around carefully to make sure no other Yahoo had seen them. My master could never understand why the Yahoos liked these stones so much, as they were useless. He told me that one day he had got a servant to take away a heap of the stones from the spot where a Yahoo

had hidden them. Finding them gone, the Yahoo howled terribly and attacked all the other Yahoos in the group. He would not eat or sleep or work until the stones were returned to the same spot. He then cheered up, but not before he had moved the stones to a more secure hiding place. The most savage Yahoo fights took place in the fields where the stones were found. Sometimes two Yahoos would spot the same stone at once and would be squabbling over it when a third one would come up and sneak off with it. My master thought this was quite like the way I had described lawyers as behaving.

Yahoos ate anything, but were fondest of things they had stolen. When they had overeaten, which was often, they would chew on a special root to make themselves sick. There was another rare root that had the same effect on them as wine did on us. After sucking it they would hug or tear at each other, howl and grin, chatter, reel about and then fall asleep in the mud.

Sometimes, young, well-fed Yahoos would be overcome with a strange disease that caused them to lie down howling and groaning in corners for no good reason. The only sure cure for this was to set them hard at work. I have noticed that a similar disease often afflicts the laziest and richest of my countrymen, and I am sure the same cure would work equally well on them.

I asked my master if I could go out and watch some Yahoos for myself. They evidently despised me, and several times I nearly fell into their clutches. I once caught a young male, about three years old. I tried to calm it, but it yelled and bit and scratched so much that I had to let it go. It had a horrible smell, like a cross between a weasel and a fox, only worse, and it covered me with its yellow excrement.

Yahoos are very agile from an early age and are strong and hardy, but cowardly. They are cunning and malicious and extremely difficult to train. The red-haired ones are the rudest and most mischievous, but also the strongest and most active.

The Houyhnhnms keep the Yahoos they are currently using in huts near the house. The rest are sent out into the fields, where they dig up roots, and

seek out carrion or catch weasels and luhimuhs (a sort of wild rat) to eat. They swim like frogs and often catch fish, which the females carry home to their young.

Once, when I was bathing in a stream, I was leapt on by a young female Yahoo. Goodness knows what would have happened if the sorrel nag, who was standing close by and keeping a watch on me, had not chased it off.

I had now spent nearly three years in the country, and had learnt quite a lot about the Houyhnhnms. These noble creatures are entirely ruled by reason and have no idea of evil. They will only state things which they know for certain are true, and so do not understand what it is to have opinions, or to argue. Their most important virtues are friendship and kindness, which they show to all the members of their race. They are always civil to each other, but do not

have any complicated ceremonies. Marriages are arranged by families and friends, and care is taken to ensure that the couple will not produce unpleasant-coloured offspring. Couples never argue or fight, and produce only one young of each sex, except for the servants, who produce three of each. If a couple should produce two males, they swap one for a foal from a couple with two females.

The young of both sexes are educated in the same way, and are taught hard work, exercise, cleanliness and moderation. They are trained by running races up and down hills and over stony ground. Four times a year they have athletics competitions. The winner's prize is a song composed in his or her praise.

Houyhnhnms do not have writing, so everything they know is handed down from mouth to mouth. However, so little happens in the country that they can easily remember everything of importance. Their calendar is based on years and months, but doesn't include weeks. They can predict eclipses of the sun but do not know any other astronomy. Their poetry is wonderful.

Their buildings are simple but well built. They make poles by taking the trunks of a certain kind of tree, which falls over when it is about forty years old, and sharpening one end with a flint. They stick the poles into the ground and weave oat-straw or wattles between them to make walls. Roofs and doors are made the same way.

Houyhnhnms use the part of the front legs just above the hoof in the same way we use our hands. They can be very skilful. I have seen a white

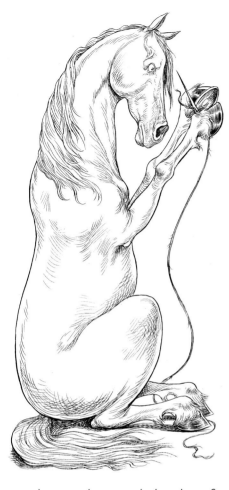

mare thread a needle which I lent her. They make stone tools out of flint, which they use to cut their hay and reap their oats.

If they do not have an accident they die only of old age, at around seventy or seventy-five years old. They become weak a few weeks before they die, and are visited by all their friends. They can usually sense when they are just about to die, and spend the last few days returning these visits, being carried on sledges drawn by Yahoos. They are buried in quiet, out-of-the-way spots and their friends and relations show no emotion when they die. I remember once my master had invited a family to visit to discuss some important business. The mare and her two children arrived very late. She apologized for her husband, who that morning had happened to lhnuwnh, which can best be translated as "retired to his first mother". She then explained that she was late because she had been discussing with her servants where to bury him. She was perfectly cheerful, and died herself about three months later.

Houyhnhnms have no word for evil but signify bad or unpleasant things by adding the word Yahoo to them. For example, a badly built house is ynholm-hnmrohlnw Yahoo.

Every four years, during spring, there is a meeting of representatives of the whole country, which lasts five or six days. One of these was held towards the end of my stay in the country. My master went as the representative of our district. At the assembly the Houyhnhnms continued debating the only subject they have ever debated, which was whether the Yahoos should be exterminated from the face of the earth or not. It was pointed out that Yahoos were the filthiest, ugliest, most pestilential and untrustworthy creatures ever known. According to tradition, they had appeared on a mountain one day, and had bred so fast that they threatened to overrun the country. To deal with the problem, the Houyhnhnms had captured them all. The older ones were killed but every Houyhnhnm kept two young ones in a kennel to use for simple tasks. It would be better if they were now got rid of and replaced by donkeys, which were much more useful.

My master then said that he had in his possession an extraordinary Yahoo, much cleverer than a normal Yahoo but still far below a Houyhnhnm. From studying me he had decided that the first Yahoos had probably come from over the sea and been left here as I had been. They had retreated to the mountains, where over the generations they had turned into the savage creatures that were present-day Yahoos.

I was very happy with my life. At my master's orders, a little room had been made for me close to his house. I plastered its walls with clay and made chairs, rush mats and mattresses of beaten hemp, which I filled with birds' feathers. When my clothes wore out, I sewed replacements out of the skins of rabbits and nnuhnohs (a small animal with a soft, downy fur). I made shoes out of wood and Yahoo skins dried in the sun. I had ample food for all my needs. Best of all, I was free of all the worries and nuisances caused by other people. I had no friends to be unreliable and no enemies to plot against me. I had no need for doctors or lawyers. I owed no one any favours. There were no pickpockets, highwaymen, gamblers, politicians, murderers, boors, cheating shopkeepers, bullies, drunkards, scoundrels, lords, fiddlers, judges or dancing teachers to disturb my peace.

My admiration for the Houyhnhnms grew and grew. I was often present when my master entertained his friends, and was sometimes even allowed to accompany him when he visited them. I of course never spoke, except in answer to the questions which he and his friends were kind enough to ask me. The more I heard them talk about humans, the more I began to despise my own race, who were obviously nothing more than jumped-up Yahoos. I disliked seeing my own reflection, as it reminded me of what I was, and began imitating the Houyhnhnms more and more in the way I walked and spoke.

Then one day disaster struck. My master gave me some terrible news. The assembly that had recently met had taken offence at the fact that my master had been treating me more like a Houyhnhnm than a mere animal. From now onwards, they decided, I should either be treated like all other Yahoos or I should be made to swim back to the place I had come from. The assembly had rejected the first idea, as they feared I would encourage the other Yahoos to revolt. Therefore I should be made to swim away. They asked my master to act on this. (They did not order him, as no Houyhnhnm ever orders another to do anything.)

I was so shocked that I fell in a dead faint at his feet. When I recovered, I said that although I could under-

stand the assembly's decision, I wished it had been a little less harsh. The nearest land was far too far away for me to swim to. Even if I did not die in the attempt, I would be forced to spend the rest of my days living amongst Yahoos. If I did have to go, I begged that I might at least be given time to build a small boat. My master agreed, and said that the sorrel nag would help me.

The boat was finished in six weeks. It was a sort of large canoe, covered with Yahoo skins. I used the soft skins of young Yahoos to make the sail, and I sealed all the cracks in the boat with Yahoo fat. When it was finished, the boat was taken to the sea in a sledge drawn by Yahoos. My master, his family and some of his friends came to see me off. I was heartbroken. As I was getting into the boat, my master was kind enough to raise a front hoof for me to kiss. I was almost overwhelmed by the honour. Having said my goodbyes, I got in the canoe and pushed off. The last thing I heard was the sorrel nag, who was very fond of me, crying out, "Hnuy illa nyha majah, Yahoo" – "Take care of yourself, gentle Yahoo."

I began my voyage on 15 February 1715. I decided that the idea of going back and living amongst Yahoos in Europe was too horrible to think about. Instead, I would find a small island where I could live alone and undisturbed. From conversations I had heard amongst the sailors before I was marooned, I thought I was probably quite near Australia, and decided to head in that direction. I eventually landed there and found a convenient spot with a supply of fresh water in a creek. I did not light a fire, being afraid that I might attract people, but lived off raw shellfish for three days. On the fourth day I wandered away from the spot and saw a group of natives around a fire. Some of them spotted me and began to come after me. I ran to my canoe, loaded up and pushed off. One of the natives fired an arrow at me, which wounded me in the left knee.

I paddled off, not sure what to do next. I was looking for another landing place when I saw a ship's sail. I could not decide whether to wait for the ship or not, but finally my loathing of Yahoos got the better of me. I turned and headed back to the spot I had come from, preferring to take my chances amongst the natives there rather than try to live with European Yahoos.

However, the ship turned out to be heading to the same creek, to collect fresh water. A group of men came ashore in a boat. They spotted my canoe and then found me lying face down behind a rock. From my strange clothes they could see that I was not a native of the region. One of them spoke to me in Portuguese and asked me who I was. I understand Portuguese very well and, standing up, said I was a poor Yahoo, banished from the Houyhnhnms. I then asked their permission to leave. They were amazed to hear me speak in their language, but didn't understand the words Yahoo and Houyhnhnm. They also fell about laughing at my voice, which, I gathered, reminded them of the neighing of a horse.

They asked me more questions. Hearing them speak was as amazing to me as if I had heard a cow or dog speak in England, or a Yahoo in Houyhnhnmland. I replied that I was an Englishman who meant them no harm, but was looking for a lonely spot where he could spend the rest of his unhappy days. They were very kind to me, and said they were sure their captain would carry me for no charge to Lisbon, where I could find a ship to take me home.

I was presented to the captain, Pedro de Mendez, a very polite and generous man. He said he would look after me and asked me what I would like to eat or drink. I was amazed to find such manners in a Yahoo, but remained silent and miserable-looking. I was ready to faint at the smell of him and his men. Finally I said I would get some food from my canoe, but instead he gave me a chicken and some excellent wine, and then ordered me to be put to bed in a clean cabin. As soon as I thought the crew were off eating, I crept out and was about to jump overboard and swim for my life. One of the crew stopped me, and I was afterwards chained up in my cabin.

After dinner Don Pedro came to me and asked why I had made such a desperate attempt to escape. I decided to treat him almost as an intelligent creature, and gave him a short account of my last voyage and my life amongst the Houyhnhnms. He obviously thought I had dreamt or imagined it all, at which I got very offended, as I had spent so long with the Houyhnhnms that I had almost forgotten what lying and invention were.

After a while Don Pedro began to believe that I might be telling the truth. However, he said that I must swear that I would not try to escape or do myself any harm before we reached Lisbon. I reluctantly agreed to his request.

He also tried to make me change out of my strange, wild clothes, and offered me his finest suit instead. I could not bear to wear anything that had been on the back of a Yahoo, but finally agreed to borrow two of his shirts, which had been recently cleaned.

We arrived at Lisbon on 5 November 1715. The captain, who had no family, allowed me to stay in his house, where I kept myself well hidden. He persuaded me to accept a newly made suit of clothes. I could not bear to have the tailor measure me, so he made them to fit Don Pedro, who was about the same size as me.

After about ten days, Don Pedro said that I should return to my wife and family, and should abandon my plan to find an isolated island where I could live alone. I finally agreed, and left Lisbon on 24 November. Don Pedro took me to the ship and lent me twenty pounds. I kept to my cabin during the voyage, pretending I was sick. We reached the Downs on 5 December and I reached my home in Redriff that afternoon.

My wife and children were filled with joy at my arrival, as they had become convinced I was dead. I'm afraid the sight of them filled me with horror and disgust – to think that I was related to these creatures! My wife kissed me, at which I was so horrified that I fainted and did not recover for nearly an hour.

# EPILOGUE

And so, dear readers, that is the story of my travels, which lasted for just over sixteen years and seven months. Of course, it is easy for those of us who travel to distant and exotic places to make things up on our return. Indeed, when I was young I was entirely taken in by many travel books which I have since discovered, to my disgust, were full of lies and fantasies. For my part, taking the noble Houyhnhnms as an example, I have decided always to stick completely to the truth.

I have, however, been told in private that I should have informed some government minister of my voyages as soon as I returned from them, as in that way England could have claimed the countries I visited as colonies.

However, I have experience of how colonists often behave. A pirate ship, for example, is blown off course and arrives at an unknown land. The pirates go ashore intending to rob whoever they find. They are greeted by friendly locals who show them generous hospitality. In return the pirates claim the country for their own king, give it a new name, murder two or three dozen of the natives and kidnap a few more to take back to their own country. Once home, they obtain a pardon from their king for their previous acts of piracy and the new land is declared a colony. More ships are quickly sent, the local people are all killed or driven away and their princes tortured to find out where they might have any gold hidden. And we call this spreading civilization.

Not surprisingly, the countries that I have described show no desire to be conquered and enslaved, or their inhabitants to be murdered or driven out of their homes. In addition none of them was rich in gold, silver, sugar, or tobacco. For these reasons, I decided that they were not worth telling our government about.

Having now answered the only possible charge against me, I hope you will let me return to my little garden at Redriff, to continue applying all the excellent lessons in behaviour taught to me by the wonderful Houyhnhnms in the education of my own family.

I will finally add that I would find it easier to get used to the company of Yahoos in general and could put up with most of their failings, horrible deformed creatures as they are, if only they were not so proud. The Houyhnhnms, of course, have no word for pride, which they would consider a terrible vice. Sadly, it is all too common amongst Yahoos and I earnestly beg any English Yahoo that has the tiniest vestige of it not to presume to appear in my sight.

*For My Parents*
M.J.

*For My Father*
C.R.

First published 2004 by Walker Books Ltd, 87 Vauxhall Walk, London SE11 5HJ

This edition published 2006

2 4 6 8 10 9 7 5 3 1

Text © 2004 Martin Jenkins   Illustrations © 2004 Chris Riddell

The right of Martin Jenkins and Chris Riddell to be identified as author and illustrator respectively of this work has been asserted by them in accordance with the Copyright, Designs and Patents Act 1988

This book has been typeset in Shinn Light

Printed in China

British Library Cataloguing in Publication Data: a catalogue record for this book is available from the British Library

ISBN-13: 978-1-4063-0174-8
ISBN-10: 1-4063-0174-4

www.walkerbooks.co.uk